# her warrior dragon

Dragon Mates
Book One

## ariel marie

# foreword

The entire Dragon Mates series written by Ariel Marie has been re-edited to enhance readers' enjoyment.

# warning

Due to the explicit language and graphic sexual scenes, this book is intended for mature (18 years +) readers only. If things of this nature offend you, this book would not be for you. If you like a good action story with hot steamy scenes with dragon shifters and their mates, then you have chosen wisely…

# Chapter One

HE CLOSED his eyes briefly and glided higher into the sky. His massive wingspan allowed him to pierce through the dense clouds as his elevation increased. Vander blew out a snort; his dragon was in full-blown battle mode, ready for combat. He loved the exhilarating feeling of gliding through the air, allowing his dragon to be in control. But tonight would not be a night of pleasurable flight.

He was on the hunt for one black dragon that had attempted to annihilate an entire farming village.

Gamair, the Death Lord, was a dragon who was pure evil, obsessed with death. Vander, The

Warrior, was a dragon shifter, and one who would put a stop to the evil monster. He would not allow the Death Lord to wreak havoc on entire communities of innocent people, all because the black dragon had nothing better to do. Vander had fought Gamair for centuries and knew most of the black dragon's tricks, but this time, he had gone too far.

Dragons had long been champions of the human race but rarely revealed themselves to the world. When they did, they used their magic to distort the human mind. To humans, dragons were a myth, a legend.

Tonight's battle of dragons would be distorted to any human who would happen to look up and see the massive creatures in the clouds.

His dragon sensed two large presences in the sky near him. He glanced around and found Jodos, his best friend since childhood, gliding next to him, while his older brother, Feno, swooped in to his right, flying alongside him. Gamair would not stand a chance on this night.

Vander turned his attention back toward the sky, only to realize he'd lost sight of Gamair. His keen eyes searched the dense clouds, but there was no sign of the black dragon.

*"There!"* Feno's voice broke through telepathically.

Vander looked in the direction of his brother's stare, and he could see the tail of the black dragon, but it disappeared again in the midst of the dense clouds.

*"I'm going up higher,"* Vander informed Jodos and Feno.

He couldn't afford to let Gamair get away. He pumped his wings, gaining momentum; he went higher, intent on finding the dragon and taking him out. If they didn't stop him soon, he would destroy more lives, and Vander would be damned if he would let that happen.

Gamair came into view, and Vander's dragon didn't hesitate. He opened his large mouth and breathed fire. Flames danced along Gamair's scales as he flew closer. The black dragon flipped out of the path of Vander's flames and threw a massive white ball of power toward him.

He tried to dodge the attack, but the energy hit Vander square in his dragon's chest. The energy paralyzed him, leaving his dragon unable to pump his wings. Both man and dragon panicked. The wind blew past his face, and his body headed toward the ground. He felt himself lose control over his dragon.

The sound of his brother's voice yelling his name filled his head, but he was unable to respond. He fell through the clouds. He knew that he was in trouble when he felt the shift begin.

*You have got to be fucking kidding me*, he thought.

His human arms appeared. His dragon left, and his full human body came forward. He blinked and let loose a curse at the speed at which he was falling.

"This is going to hurt," he muttered, and the ground rushed up, then everything went black.

———

Faye looked at the clock and groaned. She had six more hours until the end of her twelve-hour shift. The life of an emergency room nurse was rewarding but taxing on her body. Tonight was her fourth night in a row. She had picked up some extra shifts, trying to earn extra money to pay down her student loans.

Six more months of double payments, and they would be paid off. Financial freedom was her goal, and she was almost there, so this sacrifice would be well worth it. Just the thought of being free of major debt put a little more pep in her step.

She was transporting a patient who'd come

into the ER with chest pain. His tests had come back abnormal, so she had to escort him to the cath lab so that the interventional cardiologist could do an invasive test to check for blockages in the arteries surrounding his heart.

He wouldn't be coming back to the ER. He'd either go to the cardiac floor to be admitted or the operating room, if what they found warranted an emergency surgery.

"Okay, here we go, Mr. Sullivan," she said and opened the doors for Mike, the nursing assistant. She quickly followed behind and reached the side of the cart. The sounds of his heartbeat on the machines echoed down the narrow hallway.

"Thank you, Faye," Mr. Sullivan said and reached out for her hand. He was an older gentleman in his late sixties, with salt-and-pepper hair and a warm smile. The entire night, he hadn't complained, not once. It was his wife who had insisted he come to the emergency room when he had argued it was only heartburn. "I appreciate everything you've done for me."

"Oh, it's not a problem," she replied, squeezing his hand. This was why she'd become a nurse. Sometimes, patients just needed a comforting hand and a smile to help get them through the scary times. "I just want to make sure that you're good enough to get back to that pretty wife of yours," she added with a smile.

"I mean it. Don't you stop smiling," he said.

Mike wheeled him into the lab where the team of nurses and physicians were waiting.

"I won't. Now, I'm leaving you in good hands."

They quickly grabbed the monitor and exited the room with a wave so that the team could proceed with the procedure.

"What are you doing this weekend?" Mike held the door open for her.

"After I wake from my work-induced coma, I may go out with my friend, Jenna, this weekend. She's wanted to go to this bar she heard about. You and Nina have any plans?"

"I have no clue what she's planning, but me? My focus will be on the playoffs this weekend." He laughed.

Faye rolled her eyes at her coworker. She knew that Mike's wife would be dragging him out to wherever she wanted to go this weekend.

They made their way back to the emergency department and found everything calm. She enjoyed working with this team. Everyone was professional and worked together well.

"Hey, Faye!" her charge nurse, Tim, called out

from the nurses' station. "You're up for the next trauma."

"Sure thing, boss." She walked over to the nurses' station and leaned against the counter. "Just let all emergency calls know that they can only come after I grab a bite to eat and get my coffee," she joked. She batted away the balled-up paper Tim tossed at her.

"Okay. I'll let all the squads know that Faye needs a diversion until after her break," Tim said and stood.

"I knew you were my favorite charge nurse," she said in a singsong voice. She turned away from the counter and headed toward the break room.

The smell of freshly brewed coffee greeted her when she pushed the door open.

"Somebody loves me," she exclaimed and made a beeline straight for the coffee pot.

Faye grabbed her cup from the dish rack by the sink and moved the carafe out of the way before sliding her mug beneath the flow of beautiful, black, liquid gold. Coffee was a nurse's secret weapon to surviving the evening shift. Once her cup was filled, she grabbed her flavored creamer from the fridge and doctored her coffee. Who needed food when they had this liquid perfection?

Her lunch was forgotten; she grabbed the remote for the TV and sat at the table, putting her feet up. It was Friday night in Westwend, and so far, nothing much was going on. Hopefully, she could make it through the rest of her shift without any action.

In a town like Westwend, where there was a healthy mixture of the supernatural population, one never knew when things would jump off. But, tonight, she would keep her fingers crossed and pray there was no action.

"Level one trauma!" The operator's voice came through the overhead speaker.

Faye groaned. Quickly taking a healthy sip of her coffee, she paused to listen.

"ETA, five minutes."

"Shit!" she exclaimed, her feet hitting the floor. She jumped up. Hating to waste any coffee, she tried to gulp as much as she could down, but it burned the crap out of her mouth. She tossed the coffee into the sink and placed her mug on the counter.

"All I know is this person better be dying," she muttered and rushed out of the break room.

# CHAPTER TWO

"WHAT DO WE GOT?" she called out.

The man was ushered into the trauma bay. She'd been a trauma nurse for years and loved the thrill. The adrenaline rush was better than sex. Well, almost better. It had been a while, and her handy-dandy, battery-operated boyfriend was the only action she'd been seeing lately.

The first thing that caught her eye with the new patient was that he was naked. Usually, they had to cut the clothes off unconscious patients, but this one was already as naked as the day he was born.

A few of the guys in the room chuckled. They all tried to avoid his groin area, but Faye caught a peek. Her eyes widened at its size, and she swallowed hard. Whoever this guy was, he was large everywhere, and certainly blessed.

"I think we have a shifter," Moe, the paramedic answered.

One of the other nurses threw a clean sheet over the man's private area.

The team immediately got to work assessing the newcomer. The paramedic informed the room of what he knew of their patient.

"What kind of shifter?" Dr. Franks, their staff emergency room physician, asked.

"Not sure." The other paramedic shrugged. "I've never seen anything like this before."

Curiosity filled her. She hooked him up to the heart monitor, taking in his badly bruised body. It was well-toned and muscular, and the bruises covered almost every inch of his body.

*What in the world happened to him?* she wondered to herself. After she'd placed the last lead onto his chest, the sounds of his racing heartbeat filled the room.

Dr. Franks barked out orders for the crew, guiding them in their lifesaving measures. The team functioned as a well-oiled machine.

"Whatever happened to this man, being a shifter certainly saved him." Dr. Franks shook his head in awe. He stared down at the patient. "There's no way a human could have survived whatever happened to him."

"He sure is lucky." Faye hung up the telephone. Due to the patient arriving as a trauma, the radiology department bumped other patients on the schedule and were waiting to hear if they needed them. She navigated around the room and came to stand next to Dr. Franks. "I just got off the phone with radiology, and they can take him now for the CT scan."

"Good. Let's get him down there so we can make sure he doesn't have any internal damage." He nodded at her. "Page me when you all return."

"Yes, Doctor." She turned to find the other nurses, Angela and Teresa, finishing up the preparations for the trip to radiology.

"You need us to go with you?" Angela asked. She unplugged the oxygen tubing from the wall before connecting it to the portable oxygen tank on the bed.

"I don't think I need both of you. Dr. Ramsey is coming with me, and I think with Mike, we should be fine." She nodded to the ER resident.

"Yes, I'm going. I can't wait to see the images," Dr. Ramsey added.

"I'll go, Angie," Teresa volunteered. "Cover

my patients for a little bit. This shouldn't take long."

"No problem," Angela said with a salute. She disappeared from the room.

Faye turned back to her patient and sighed. This was going to be a long night. "Let's roll out."

————

"One hundred and fifty bones are fractured." Dr. Franks stared at the bedside computer screen.

"That's almost all of his bones," Faye gasped. She finished hanging a new bag of intravenous fluid for the John Doe. Her eyes flew to the patient who had yet to awaken. It was like someone had picked him up and thrown him from a very high building.

Who could survive something so traumatic?

There was no other explanation for how he had so many broken bones. Someone didn't want this man to live.

"There's nothing we can do right now but wait." Dr. Franks shook his head. "The only explanation for why he's still alive is that he's a shifter, and as a shifter, he'll just need time, and his body will heal itself."

"Should we consult orthopedics?" Dr. Ramsey asked.

"Not right now. Let's see what he's like in the morning. Shifters' bodies heal rather quickly. We'll rescan him in the morning..." Dr. Franks voice faded as the two physicians stepped out of the room, leaving Faye alone with her charge.

She logged in to the computer to chart a few things on her patient. The intensive care unit didn't have an open bed right now, so it seemed like he would be with them in the emergency room for a little while longer. A noise grabbed her attention, and she paused her typing, glancing over at the man. She walked over to him and was finally able to get a good look at him.

She tilted her head to the side, trying to get past the bruising, and she could see he was handsome. Very handsome, now that she was studying him closer. He could be downright gorgeous. His dark hair was just long enough for a girl to glide her fingers through. He had long eyelashes that any woman would pay big money to get. And his chest—

She had to dart her eyes away and catch her breath. What was the matter with her?

"Who are you?" she whispered. She reached out and moved his dark hair from his face. She adjusted the oxygen tubing in his nose and saw her hands were shaking. She didn't understand why, but she was absolutely captivated by him. "What are you?"

She jumped; his eyes fluttered. She pulled her hand away quickly, embarrassed at almost getting caught touching him. He released a groan, and his eyes opened. His golden irises mesmerized her.

*He is definitely a shifter.*

"Come closer," he moaned, his eyes shutting tight.

With her heart beating erratically, she leaned in, barely able to hear what he was saying.

"What is it? Are you okay? Do you need something?" she whispered frantically.

He took a deep breath, and she waited to hear what he was about to say. Would he whisper his last dying words? Who would she contact to tell that he'd died and that he'd left his last request with her? She was two seconds from hitting the code button, waiting for him to speak.

"You smell so good," he murmured.

"What?" She drew back in shock, taking in the large grin that had spread across his face. "Are you serious?" she sputtered, unable to believe that she thought he was dying, and he was sniffing her.

"You do smell good. I couldn't wait for those doctors to leave the room," he announced, his eyes filled with a devious glint.

Oh, without the bruises, he would be one hot panty-melting shifter. She swallowed hard and took a few steps away from the bed. She had heard plenty of stories of shifters and knew she should stay far away from him. Who wanted nights filled with hot, unbridled passion? Multiple orgasms? What woman would want sexual satisfaction that no human man could match?

Nope, not her, she tried to convince herself, but failed. And the look he was giving her now told her that he wanted to swallow her whole. Her body released a shudder with just the thought of him tasting her.

"So, let me get this straight. You've been awake this whole time?" She stomped her foot with her hand on her waist.

"I woke up when I was in that machine," he said and attempted to stretch his arms out but stopped and winced.

She watched, amazed, as he slowly sat up. He grimaced slightly, turning, setting his feet on the floor.

"You shouldn't be getting up." She rushed to his side, his flirtation forgotten, the nurse in her kicking in. "Almost every single bone in your body is broken!"

"I'll be fine," he brushed her off. He tore the oxygen tubing from his nose and turned to her.

The slow perusal of his eyes, starting at her feet, then up toward her eyes, left her squirming. Her body betrayed her, and a slight hint of moisture formed at the apex of her thighs.

*Down girl*, she thought to herself. *He's a patient*, she chanted in her mind. But it didn't do any good. Even though he was beat up and bruised, she was still attracted to him. No way would she get involved with a patient. She brushed her hair from her eyes and promised herself a date with her B.O.B as soon as she got home.

# CHAPTER THREE

"SO, FAYE, IS IT?" Vander asked. He stared at the gorgeous nurse.

She nodded and returned his gaze.

If he had known nurses looked like this at the local hospital, he would have visited more often. Everything about her, from her dark hair in a messy bun on top of her head, to her hospital scrubs that didn't hide her deliciously curvy frame, turned him on. Just sitting in her presence made him forget about chasing after Gamair. Vander hadn't realized he had a thing for nurses. Sexy nurses were moving to the top of his list right now.

He held back a grimace, trying not to show the

pain that racked his body. The doctor had said he had one hundred and fifty bones broken. That had to be a new record for him. The dragon in him had forced him to awaken during his healing slumber, where he had found himself in that machine. He'd heard her speaking to someone in the room. Her voice had called to his dragon.

It wanted her as much as a dragon wanted a hoard full of gold and treasure.

*And have her, we will.*

"You're going to do more damage," she announced. "Let me call the doctor." She turned to reach for a phone that rested on her portable computer cart.

"No." He shook his head. He wouldn't need a doctor. There was nothing the human doctor could do for him. He just needed to rest and allow his body to heal. With this amount of damage, it would take a couple of days to heal. "Take this stuff off of me." He pointed to all of the wires and tubing that flowed around him.

"I can't. You're in the hospital. Whatever you did or was done to you, could have killed you."

He snorted at her little speech. He was a powerful dragon shifter—Vander, The Warrior. It would take more than falling twenty thousand feet to kill him. He peeled a sticker from his chest and held back a grimace upon moving his left arm. The damn thing must be broken. Sweat formed on his forehead at his movements.

"If I take everything off you, will you promise not to die on me?" she asked, her hands on her hips.

Vander paused what he was doing and glanced over at her. He had known her for mere minutes, and he already loved her irritated look. The way her brows drew together and her eyes narrowed on him had his dragon huffing.

"Yes," he promised. He wouldn't be dying today. Dragon shifters lived for centuries. He was a dragon in his prime and had many years left on this planet. Falling out of the sky was not the way to kill a dragon. Not many knew how dragons could be killed; that was a secret kept close to their kind only.

"Fine. I'll do it," she muttered, coming to stand in front of him. "I swear, if you die, I will kill you myself!"

"I love your sass." He threw her a wink.

She avoided his eyes and quickly removed all the stickers from his chest. The alarms in the room sounded as she peeled the last one off.

"Everything okay in there?" a voice came in over the speaker.

"Yes, I got it. Can you pause the alarms for room twenty-three, please?" Faye asked the voice. She hit a button on the IV pump.

"Got it," the voice answered.

He waited patiently. She continued working on freeing him. He took advantage of her closeness to study her features. Her eyes—green, with flecks of hazel—were beautiful. The small mole on the edge of her top lip had him wanting to lick it and explore her mouth thoroughly with his tongue. He didn't realize that he had been holding his breath while he looked his fill.

His dragon stood at attention. She moved away from him. It wanted her near him again.

"All done, Mister...wait, what is your name?"

"Vander," he answered with another grimace. The pain was kicking in for real now. He drew in a deep breath and blew it out, trying to fight the draw to sleep. His body was now telling him he would need to rest. The healing slumber would draw him into a deep, undisturbed stasis, which would allow his body to heal on its own.

"Mr. Van—" she started.

He cut her off with a raised hand. He needed to hear her say his name. The animal in him rumbled deep in his chest.

"My surname is Kelmyar, but you can call me

by my given name, Vander." His eyes locked on hers, waiting to hear her say it. *Soon*, he promised himself, *she will be screaming my name*. He couldn't wait for that moment. But, for now, he needed to rest. He would need to be in top shape for when he had her.

"Vander, please, let me help you back into the bed," she insisted, a worried look plastered on her face.

Sweat poured down his face, and he figured she was probably worried he would pass out or something. He nodded, knowing when to admit to defeat.

He released a hiss; she gently grabbed his legs to help swing them back into the bed, then pulled the blankets over him. He took a few deep breaths, trying to slow his racing heart.

"Get some rest." She patted his hand gently.

He grabbed her hand when she moved to turn away.

"There's room for one more in here," he offered with his winning smile. Women usually flocked to him when he offered *'the smile.'* No woman could resist the Vander charm.

"You're persistent, aren't you?" She tilted her head to the side. Her eyes took him in, quickly sweeping the entire bed before meeting his.

He was having a hard time keeping his eyes open; the healing slumber was upon him.

"I see something that I want, I go after it," he mumbled, his eyes drooping.

"Well, in this position, honey, you wouldn't be able to handle me."

He smiled. Sleep overcame him. God, he loved her sass. Wait until he healed properly, she wouldn't know what hit her. Vander, The Warrior, was going to go after his woman, but for now, he would sleep.

# CHAPTER FOUR

IT WAS FINALLY THE WEEKEND, and Jenna had dragged Faye out to the club she had been dying to go to. Faye followed closely behind Jenna who pulled her to the bar. Jenna's curly blonde hair flowed down her back and bounced with the sway of her body as she bopped her head to the song playing. Faye smiled at her friend. Jenna was a person who enjoyed a good time and made sure that Faye did, too. She always complained that Faye worked too much and didn't relax enough. They had been best friends since junior high and were as close as sisters.

Jenna was determined to make sure Faye had a good time, and after working all the shifts that she had been working, she had no intention of resisting. She didn't even remember the name of the club they were in, but that didn't matter. Jenna knew the bouncer, and he let them in with no wait.

Popular music blared through the speakers, and the dance floor was packed with bodies, grinding against each other in sync with the beat. They finally made their way to the bar and found two seats.

"What do you want? My treat!" Jenna shouted in her ear.

"Whatever! It doesn't matter!" Faye shouted back.

Jenna nodded and waved to get the bartender's attention. Faye rotated her chair so she could people-watch. Sometimes, it was her favorite part of going out. Watching sloppy drunk people try to dance always gave her hours of entertainment.

"Here!" Jenna handed her a double shot of a clear liquid. Her friend knew her well.

*Vodka.*

"Thanks!" Faye mouthed. With the blaring music her friend wouldn't be able to hear her.

"Girls' night out!" Jenna shouted and held her glass in the air.

"Hear, hear!" Faye smiled.

Their glasses clinked together in honor of their first night out in a while, before they both tipped back their drinks.

Faye winced slightly at the burning sensation of the cool drink. She was ready to relax and have a good time.

"Let's dance!" Jenna motioned to the dancers.

"What the hell!" Placing the empty glass on the bar, Faye hopped down from the chair.

Tonight, she was dressed to party. She was feeling sexy in her four-inch heels and short black dress that displayed her bare back, highlighting her curvy body. She was a thick girl and wasn't afraid to show off her curves. She left her hair to fall in waves down her back and kept her makeup natural.

She knew there were eyes on her and Jenna. They made their way to the dance floor. The pin-prickly sensation that crept along the exposed skin of her back was proof. She looked around and entered the throng of dancers, but she didn't see anyone staring at her. A popular slow song came on, and they both laughed, singing along and dancing to the beat.

Nights like this were a stress relief for Faye. She was starting to feel herself relax and knew the shot of alcohol was doing its job. It had been a while since she'd been able to let her hair down.

She felt a presence behind her as she swayed to the beat. A warm body brushed her from behind. The alcohol was her liquid courage to continue dancing. He pulled her back to him. Her body melted on his. She had a fleeting thought that they were too close, but for some reason, she couldn't force herself to draw away.

She glanced at Jenna, who gave her a wide grin and a thumbs-up.

"He's hot!" she mouthed.

The crowd shifted, and Jenna was tugged away. Faye scanned the dancers, but she could only catch a glimpse of her friend.

Her eyes closed for a brief second, lost in the music, and the feel of his warm breath gliding across the crook of her neck. He left a trail of light kisses along her skin, her nipples aching, pushing into her bra. They begged to be set free, wanting to feel the roughness of his hands on them. She held in a groan; his hardened length brushed the swell of her ass.

Who was this guy who practically had her losing all decency in a nightclub?

Curiosity got the best of her. She had to know who this guy was turning her on with just his body. *A magnificently sculpted body, from the feel of him against my back.* She slowly swung herself around, still trapped in his arms, with a smile on her face.

She froze in place and stared into familiar golden irises.

It was him!

Vander.

The mysterious shifter from the hospital. He had disappeared from the hospital two days after he was brought in, and now, there he stood in front of her in a crisp white button-down and dark slacks, looking as if nothing had ever happened to him.

A wide grin spread across his face, and she knew she had been right.

He was downright gorgeous without all the bruises. She couldn't even speak and gazed up at him. Her hands slowly found their way up to his face, touching all the places she knew had once held a bruise.

He guided her body in a sensual dance that was in sync with the beat of the music, crushing her aching breasts to his solid chest. Her breath caught in her throat; his lips covered hers. The dancers surrounding them faded off into the back, and she groaned. Her fingers reached up and dove into his hair. It was just as thick as she had imagined it to be.

He tasted of peppermint. His tongue pushed its way into her mouth, coaxing hers to duel with his. She didn't know if he had placed a magic spell over her, but she wanted to reach up and rip his shirt from his body, just so she could feel the muscles beneath her fingertips. It had to be magic making her feel this way, or maybe it was the alcohol. She didn't normally try to jump a guy's bones in the middle of a crowded dance floor. She didn't know what was coming over her, but right now, she knew that she wanted him.

She couldn't fight it.

He had been on her mind constantly since he'd woken up as her patient. This large, mysterious man had plagued her dreams for days. When she had returned to work to find him gone, she had been disappointed.

His large hands cupped her cheeks, and he gently pulled back, placing a chaste kiss to her lips.

"Faye," he murmured.

"What are you doing here?" she whispered.

Someone bumped into her back. She looked around and noticed that everyone else was moving to an upbeat song, and they were the only two dancing to their own slow beat.

"I told you, when I see something that I want, I go after it."

"That's crazy! You barely know me!" she exclaimed. Her heart slammed against her chest. He couldn't be serious.

"I know all I need to know," he replied. He gripped her hand in his and brought it up to his chest. His eyes practically glowed, and he stared down at her.

She didn't know what type of shifter he was, but she was drawn to him. She wanted to fight what she was feeling, but she was losing the battle.

"You're crazy," she said. She glanced around, but there was no sign of Jenna in the throng of dancers. Some kind of a best friend she was. "Did you put a spell over me or something?"

"No." He shook his head. His eyes had yet to leave hers.

She bit her lip. His golden irises mesmerized her.

"I cannot control your thoughts or feelings. It's destiny. I feel it, too."

"I'm not a supernatural. I'm just a human." Faye shook her head. She didn't have any powers, and destiny certainly didn't hold anything in store for humans. She was just a regular human, nothing special about her, but his next words stopped her in her tracks.

"Come home with me."

"I can't—" she started.

He cut her off with a finger to her lips.

"Please," he murmured and leaned in close, replacing his finger with his lips.

She melted into the kiss, and all thoughts went out of the window.

"Okay."

# CHAPTER FIVE

VANDER GUIDED Faye behind him and made his way out of the club. Her smaller hand gripped his tight. They took a few steps to the curb. His car should be pulling up any minute. He didn't need to use magic to find her. Thanks to social media, he knew where she was going to be tonight. One search of her name, and he'd found her on the popular network, posting where she was going with her friend.

Two days of slumber had allowed his body to heal. The moment he'd awoken, he'd walked straight out of the hospital. Once he had made it to a clearing in the woods, he'd shifted into his magnificent dragon and flown home, high up in the mountains, to plan the claiming of his mate.

He knew she could feel the pull. The way her body responded to his let him know his dragon had been right—she belonged to them.

Drunken partiers spilled out from the club. Faye gripped his arm with both of her hands, and he drew her in close, tucking her into him, just as James, his driver, parked the dark sedan at the curb.

"Come on," he said, opening the back door for her.

He couldn't wait to get her to his home, where he could peel the tiny black dress from her curvy body. He climbed into the backseat behind her and shut the door, closing them off from the world. The partition was up, leaving them completely alone. Their bodies rocked gently with the car moving away from the curb.

"Wow," she murmured, looking around the inside before her gaze settled on his eyes.

The interior was dark, but his dragon sight allowed him to see her. The car made a turn, and her body fell and bumped into his.

His dragon roared for them to take her. His fingers itched with the need to have her in his arms.

"Sorry," she mumbled.

He shifted his arm and tucked her into his side, and her small hand settled on his chest. He held his breath; her petite fingers danced along the buttons of his shirt. He turned his head and breathed out, settling his chin on the top of her head, then breathed in her scent. It was addicting.

Her fingers trailed their way down his abdomen. His cock jumped to attention at the temptation of her fingers. When she reached his belt and undid the buckle, he threaded his fingers through her thick mane and eased her head back. She gasped, and he covered her mouth with his.

He had wanted to wait until they got back to his place, where he could lay her out across his oversized bed. The feel of her fingers diving beneath his boxer briefs took his breath away; her hand found its way to his hardened length.

He growled against her lips. She moved her hand up and down his cock. Vander scooped her up and placed her across his lap, his hands disappearing beneath her dress. They met the little scrap of material that was supposed to be her panties. The sound of material ripping filled the air as he tore it away, freeing her body.

Her mouth found his again in a frantic kiss. He didn't know how she'd managed to pull his cock out, but she did. His sexy little nurse was filled with fire, and he loved it.

She hovered above him, and he lined the head of his cock at her soaked entrance. He groaned, the proof of her readiness coating the tip of his length. The car jerked, hitting a pothole, and sent her sliding down onto him, hard.

"Oh God," she screamed, wrapping her arms around him.

Vander cursed beneath his breath at the feel of her tightness gripping him. Her walls held on to him, and he gripped her ass tight and said every prayer he knew to keep from blowing early.

He had to move.

The gentle sway of the car assisted them in setting a rhythm. He lifted her and slowly brought her down onto him. His hardened length swelled even more at the tight fit. She may be small, but she was able to accept him with no problem.

Sweat dripped from his temples. He restrained himself and his beast. His dragon was ready to mark her, to make her theirs.

*Not yet.*

Not in the back of a vehicle. The day he claimed her, the most precious of jewels and pure silk sheets would surround her. She would have the finest things in life that he had collected over the years. He could easily imagine her in nothing but a diamond dragon's eye on her neck, nestled down between her plump mounds.

His dragon rumbled deep within his chest at the image that was broadcasted through his mind.

"Vander," she moaned, her voice breaking through his thoughts. She tightened her arms around him, crushing her breasts to him.

He needed her fully naked and was tempted to rip her dress off, but he had to remember that they were in the car.

"Faye, stay with me tonight," he demanded. This one time in the car would not be enough. He wanted to get her back to his condo. His eyes locked on to hers before her head rolled back. Her eyes were shut tight, and he slammed her down on his cock.

"Vander," she chanted repeatedly.

Their pace picked up. He paused, wanting to get her attention.

He reached down and found her sensitive nub with his thumb.

"Tell me you'll stay with me tonight," he demanded again and applied pressure to her clit. He massaged her slick nub with intense force. He knew he wasn't playing fair, but when he wanted something, he went after it, and didn't care what he had to do to get it.

"Yes," she groaned, moving her hips in tandem with his thumb.

"All night?" he asked. He would be relentless until he was sure that he got want he wanted.

"Yes," she screamed.

Her orgasm washed over her. Her muscles surrounded his cock, pulsated, the sensations hitting her. Her small body trembled against his.

Vander roared. Unable to hold off anymore, he released her nub so he could thrust his hips, pushing his cock deeper into her core. The familiar tingling sensation zipped through his body, and he released his seed deep inside her.

His breaths came fast and hard, and she slumped against him. He cradled her to his chest with his semi-hard cock still buried within her.

They'd have to discuss birth control later. Vander knew that as a dragon shifter, he would only be able to impregnate his mate once they'd mated. Later, he'd have to explain everything to her. The mating ceremony, and the need for her to consume at least an ounce of his blood every year to give her the life longevity needed to mate with a dragon shifter for life.

The car drew to a halt. He opened his eyes and

peered out the window to find them in the private garage of his apartment building.

"We're here," he rested his chin on top of her head.

Her response was muffled by his chest, her body lying limp against him.

"Say again?" He chuckled.

"I'm not going to be able to walk," she mumbled and turned her head to the side.

"Don't worry." He pushed her hair away from her face. "I got you."

And he did. Now that he had her in his arms, he would never let her go.

## CHAPTER SIX

FAYE WOKE to the softest material she had ever felt. It slid across her naked skin as she turned on her side. The plushness of the bed held her hostage and refused to let her go. She was okay with staying there. She had muscles on her that she didn't even know could be sore.

All thanks to Vander.

She smiled and buried her face into her pillow.

She had lost track of how many times he had made her come. She had never been with a lover before who took such care of her and ensured she reached her peak every single time.

She released a giggle and tried to remember if

she ever had so many orgasms in one night, but for the life of her, she couldn't think of one time.

Not one.

"Good morning," a familiar deep voice rumbled beside her. The bed dipped from Vander's weight. He sat on the edge of the bed near her.

She rolled in his direction, bringing the silk sheet with her to keep her naked form covered. Shyness overcame her, and she stared into his golden eyes.

Now that it was the light of day, it meant their passion-filled night would come forward in the light of day. It wasn't a dream or fantasy but a reality. She had to face the man who'd made her climax repeatedly with his tongue, fingers, and cock.

"Morning." She smiled and settled back against the plush pillows.

He had thrown on a pair of sweatpants but remained shirtless, displaying his well-defined chest and ridges of his abdomen. Memories of her tongue tracing every one of those ridges flashed before her eyes.

Her core clenched with just the memory of the saltiness of his skin. Unconsciously, her tongue came out and licked her bottom lip, as if tasting him again. His golden eyes darkened, and they followed her tongue's movement.

*Down girl*, she thought to herself. What was wrong with her? She was turning into a horn ball from just one night with Vander.

"I have something for you." He chuckled, as if reading her mind.

She knew if he just gave the word, she would be tearing the sheet off herself for another round with the man.

The divine smell of bacon hit her, and her stomach rumbled. She glanced around Vander and saw a tray filled with food sitting on the oversized nightstand.

Okay, after she ate, she would tear the sheet off her body and drag him back into bed with her. There was no way she could pass up on breakfast. A girl needed sustenance to keep up her stamina.

Didn't she?

"I see," she said, sitting up higher. "Breakfast in bed? You didn't have to do that."

"I've kept you occupied all night. It was the least I could do," he replied with his devilish smile. He leaned in and placed a chaste kiss upon her lips. "But I have something else for you besides the food."

"Oh?" She cocked an eyebrow at him. Food

was good enough. What else could he possibly have for her?

She watched him reach over and pull open the top drawer of the nightstand. His hand disappeared inside, and he brought out a black velvet square box.

She gasped as he handed it to her.

"What is this?" she exclaimed. Her hands shook, and she held it before her. "I can't accept this." She shook her head and thrust it toward him.

"You haven't even looked inside." He pushed the box back to her.

Her face must have given away her true feelings. She was hurt. Did he really think she would require payment for the night they'd shared? She wasn't a prostitute, for Pete's sake!

"No one thinks you're a prostitute, Faye," Vander assured her softly.

Her eyes flew to him. Could he read her mind?

He placed his hand over hers and stared deep into her eyes. "From the moment I woke up to find you over me, I knew that there was something special about you. What's in that box is yours. Think of it as a gift for taking care of me when I was in the hospital." He pushed the box gently toward her again. "Now, open it."

She looked up at him one last time and fiddled with the box. Her breath caught in her throat, and she slowly opened it. Tucked amongst a dark satin cloth was one of the most beautiful necklaces she had ever seen. It was a purple, amethyst dragon's eye pendant, with oxidized brass surrounding it. She gasped at the beautiful amethyst with crystal clear diamonds surrounding the eye.

Her eyes flew to Vander.

"It's a special piece. It represents me and my kind," he murmured and tucked a strand of her hair behind her ear. "I want you to have it."

His kind?

Holy hell.

Her mouth flopped open in disbelief.

"Wait! Are you telling me that you're a—"

She couldn't bring herself to say it. She thought they didn't exist, except only in bedtime stories that parents told their children. Her eyes widened, and she stared into his beautiful golden eyes. He smiled slightly at her shocked expression.

"Dragon shifter." He nodded, watching her carefully.

It explained everything.

*How he had broken almost all the bones in his body.* He'd literally fallen to the earth.

*His quick recovery*. Dragon shifters were one of the most powerful shifters ever.

*Him tracking her down*. Dragons loved to hoard what they claimed as theirs.

*The beautiful gift*. Dragons loved to bestow expensive gifts on the ones they cared for.

"But I thought dragon shifters were a myth," Faye whispered. She glanced down at the beautiful pendant.

"We have been around for centuries. We only allow those we want to see us." He tipped her face up to him and placed a gentle kiss on her lips. "Let me help you put this on."

She nodded, anxious to see what it would look like on her. He took the box from her, and she turned slightly away from him. She lifted her hair from her neck and gently placed the pendent on her. It settled just above her breasts.

"I want to see it." She laughed and stared down. She wrapped the sheet around her then jumped from the bed. Smiling, she raced across the room to the floor-length mirror, the sheet dragging behind her.

She gasped loudly and gazed at herself in the mirror, patting down her crazed bed head, assessing herself. Her face was relaxed, with a sexy, satisfied grin plastered across it. Her gaze trailed down and locked on the pendant.

It was perfect.

"It would be better with you naked," he murmured and came up behind her.

His strong arms engulfed her from behind, and he brought her body flush against his. Her heart sped up, and he unfolded the sheet from around her, allowing it to fall to the floor. Her nipples hardened, the chilled air caressing them, drawing them into tiny buds. His eyes darkened, and he took in her naked form.

She moaned, her body quickly responding to his.

"Yes," he hissed. "Much better."

## CHAPTER SEVEN

VANDER STALKED through his castle toward the sunroom, where Feno and Jodos waited for him. His weekend had been spent locked up in his city condo with Faye. His dragon hated leaving her, but he had to attend to business. Hunting down Gamair was still a top priority.

"Gentlemen," he greeted them and burst through the door. He knew his brother hated to be kept waiting, but Faye was worth any ass chewing from his older sibling.

"It's about damn time," Feno growled from where he paced by the oversized window.

His brother shot him a stern look as he walked

toward him. Vander held out his hand, which his brother grasped in a firm handshake.

"Hello to you, too, big brother." Vander chuckled.

Feno walked over to the couch. Vander could tell his brother was pissed because he grumbled under his breath. Vander caught the words, "no respect" and took a seat on the couch.

"And how is your female?" Jodos asked and slapped him on the back.

"She's everything that I could imagine," he admitted, memories of the weekend flashing before his eyes. His favorite part was seeing her naked with only his pendant on, just as he had dreamed she would look. The real deal proved to be much better than anything he could have ever imagined. His dragon huffed at the thought that she now wore their pendant, which symbolized that she was to be protected by them.

"Mother would be proud that you have found your mate. When will the mating ceremony be?" Feno asked with a raised eyebrow.

Vander paused. He hadn't shared with Faye that she was his mate. He'd told a slight fib when he'd told her the dragon eye was just a gift. It wasn't just any gift but a symbol of his claim on her.

"We hadn't made it that far," Vander admitted sheepishly. He took a seat in his oversized recliner.

"Oh?"

Feno and Jodos shared a quick look. Vander wasn't worried. He knew she was just as crazy about him as he was her. There was no rush. They could take their time. He had certain matters to take care of first, and then she would be his.

"She's a human. She's not accustomed to our ways. We have plenty of time. Once we destroy Gamair, there will be nothing standing in my way of claiming her."

"Sounds like a good plan." Feno nodded and relaxed against the couch.

A dragon always protected their mate to the death. His beast was ready to prepare the castle for her arrival, and it had to be perfect for her. Everything that he possessed would be hers. Over his long life, he had collected precious jewels, priceless artworks, and more money than any human could possibly need.

It would all be hers.

"After you went down, I followed him going north, toward Canada," Jodos began.

Vander knew Gamair loved to hide in the remote mountainous regions of the northern country. There were many dense areas of the country that were favorites of many dragons, due to the remote locations and low human populations.

"And while you were playing the helpless patient in the hospital, I spoke to a few of the farmers from the village," Feno advised.

"How are they?" Vander leaned forward. It was because of the destruction of Gamair that these people were displaced and had to start over.

"They're shaken up, but they're resilient. They're prepared to rebuild their community."

"Whatever they need, we will supply," Vander volunteered. They would help the peaceful human community rebuild and prosper. "Whatever the cost."

———

"What are you doing today?" Angela asked as they left the break room.

Unfortunately, Faye had to return to reality. Her weekend with Vander had been amazing, but she couldn't stay in bed with the dragon shifter forever. Reality waited for her when she returned home. She had bills to pay and a life to lead.

Memories of him walking her to her door burst forth. The kiss that he'd given her left her knees weak. He made her promise that he could see her again, but there was no need to even think on it. Her immediate answer was yes.

Of course she wanted to see him again.

His pendent weighed heavy against her chest; it fit snug beneath her scrub top. He insisted that she never remove it. As beautiful as it was, she had no problem keeping that promise.

"My couch is calling me." She laughed, thinking that she had barely gotten any sleep, thanks to Vander. Today, when she got off work, she would be catching up on some much-needed sleep. She was still running off adrenaline and her excitement. "My blanket and the couch will be my best friend as soon as I get home."

The operator's voice broke through the intercom, announcing a trauma was on the way to the hospital. They both took off jogging back toward the emergency department. Faye wasn't happy that someone's life was in danger, but it looked as if the rest of the shift would fly by for her. A few more hours, and she would be homebound.

The medics met them in the bay area with the latest trauma patient. Working a coding patient was second nature to Faye. In their town, the hospital stayed busy, and she had enough experience with the acutely ill patients. The team worked tirelessly on the motor vehicle accident victim, but unfortunately, the man did not survive.

Losing a patient was never easy for Faye, but she believed if it was a person's time to go, no amount of human intervention would change that.

"I'm going out for a breather," Faye announced. She spun on her heel and left from the room. She just needed to clear her mind from the past hour. The patient was young, and they had worked on him for a long time in hopes that they would be able to bring him back, but they were unsuccessful.

"I'm coming with you," Teresa announced and followed behind Faye. "I need a fucking smoke after that."

"Sure," Faye muttered. She walked down the hallways of the hospital that led to the back.

She had wanted a few minutes by herself, just to clear her mind. The sound of his wife's tortured scream echoed through her head, when the physician had informed her that her husband didn't make it.

"Wow, look at those stars," Teresa exclaimed.

They exited the hospital. The smoke hut was set away from the building, giving employees and visitors a place to smoke. It reminded her of a bus stop, only those sitting inside were waiting for their next nicotine fix.

"It is beautiful." Faye stared at the clear dark sky. Not a cloud was in sight, just the twinkle of stars lining the beautiful canvas of night. "Hey, I'm going to sit over here," she motioned to a bench outside the hut. She hated the smell of cigarette smoke and didn't want to chance it getting on her while her friend lit up.

She plopped down on the bench and breathed a sigh of relief. The faint tinge of cigarette smoke lingered in the air. Teresa sat quietly, enjoying her nicotine fix.

"You all right out there?" Teresa's voice broke through the quiet.

"Yeah, I'm good," Faye replied and closed her eyes for a brief moment.

She would be all right. Not only was this a part of nursing, but it was a part of life. Everyone had to die at some point. No one lived forever.

A cool breeze drifted by, calming her nerves, but it didn't last long. The hairs on the back of her neck rose; an uncomfortable feeling overcame her. A light noise caught her attention. She opened her eyes and found a dark, menacing figure standing near the entrance of the building.

Faye's eyes locked on him, while her body

froze in place. She squinted at the figure, trying to see if it was an employee of the hospital, but no one who had to wear a suit would be at the hospital at this time of night.

"Can I help you?" she called out. She reached down into the pocket of her scrubs and was comforted by the feel of her cellphone.

"Just needed some fresh air," the deep voice answered.

His excuse still didn't sit well with her. In order to exit the building from that door, the person would have had to swipe out of the building. Thanks to the hospital's security, employees had to swipe in and out of certain doors. If he had walked from the other side of the hospital, she would have heard his footsteps.

Red flags.

"Who the hell is that?" Teresa asked from the hut's entrance.

"Someone who needed air," Faye replied, not taking her eyes off the figure. She made a mental note to complain to the higher-ups of the hospital about better lighting in the area. The once-serene feeling she had was gone, and she was left feeling creeped out.

"You're Faye Adams, aren't you?" he asked and slowly made his way to her.

Oh, hell no. Time to call security.

"Don't come any closer," she shouted and pulled her phone from her pocket.

"There's no use in calling anyone," he warned, still walking toward her.

"What in the—?" She tried hitting the screen of her smartphone, but it remained black. It was as if it had gone dead, but she distinctly remembered charging it earlier. "Hey, do you have your phone?"

She turned to her friend but let loose a scream. Teresa was frozen in place, staring unblinking at the figure.

"As I said, it's useless calling for help. No one would be able to hear you." His haughty voice floated through the air.

"What do you want from me?" she hardened her voice. She hoped that she gave off the appearance that she was unafraid of him. But, to be honest, she was scared shitless and prayed her voice didn't shake.

"Feisty *and* beautiful. I love it. No wonder Vander is smitten with you." He came to stand near her.

She braced herself, ready to run if she needed to.

She could finally make out his features. He was

tall and well-dressed. His suit was tailored perfectly to him, denoting a body that was well taken care of. His dark hair was combed back perfectly from his face. Even with the slight breeze blowing, his hair didn't budge.

With all of the bad vibes radiating from the man, Faye didn't want to admit to anything, especially to knowing Vander. The man in front of her was pure evil. It didn't take a psychic to realize it.

"Who?"

"Don't play coy with me." He chuckled. He stood there and placed his hands in his pockets.

"I'm not sure what you're speaking of."

"Keep trying to deny it, but I know the truth. I also know that he will never be able to stop me, but I want you to do me a favor."

"What would that be?" she asked wearily. She glanced at Teresa, who was still frozen in the same spot. Faye's heart rate increased, her fear mounting.

Whoever, or whatever he was, he was powerful. Who could just freeze someone?

"Tell him to cease his pursuit of me," he said and turned, walking away.

"Or what?" she asked. She just had to know. Was he like Vander? Was he a dragon shifter, too?

"He will lose something of extreme value."

She blinked, and he was gone. How the hell could he have disappeared into thin air?

"What's going on?" Teresa asked.

Faye turned to her friend with her eyes wide. Teresa looked at her, patiently waiting for an answer, but Faye just stared at her in shock. It dawned on her that Teresa had no recollection that she had been frozen in place. There was no way that Faye could tell her, though. She would never believe it. She glanced back to where the stranger had stood and still didn't see any sign of him in the parking lot.

What the hell?

## CHAPTER EIGHT

VANDER'S DRAGON blew out a frustrated breath. There was no sign of Gamair anywhere. He coasted through the Canadian mountainous region, but nothing. It was like he had disappeared off the face of the planet. But Vander knew his enemy would be hiding somewhere. They would have to broaden their search in the hunt of the Death Lord.

*"Any luck?"* Feno's voice broke through Vander's thoughts.

Feno and Jodos were checking out other parts of the vast northern country. Gamair would only be able to hide for so long before they found him.

*"Fuck no,"* Vander responded. Frustrated, he

angled his dragon's body to turn around in order to head back home. Someone back in the States would make him feel better.

*Faye.*

Just the thought of her smile had his wings pumping faster as he cut through the dense clouds. Just the thought of being near her again made his heart pound and his dragon desperate to get to her.

The memory of the softness of her skin, the taste of her lips, and the smell of her slick folds increased his dragon's speed.

*"Are you changing course?"* Feno asked.

*"Yeah, there's no sign of him,"* Vander replied telepathically. *"I'm going to head back to town."*

A slight twinge in his gut caught his attention. Something was wrong. Once a dragon identified a mate, they would always be in tune with them. The dragon would always be able to feel their emotions, and right now, the slight hint of fear tingled along his spine. He knew *he* wasn't afraid of anything, so what he was experiencing could only be what Faye was feeling, and something had her frightened.

*"Off to see your mate? She can wait. We need to find this fucker,"* Feno huffed.

*"Believe me, big brother, we will find him, but I*

*need to get back to Faye. Something is wrong."* Vander's dragon was one of the swiftest in all the land and would make it back to her in record time.

*"Go to her,"* Feno ordered.

He didn't need to be told twice. He knew that his brother and Jodos would hunt down Gamair.

He drew closer to Westwend and needed to find a place to land his massive-sized dragon and shift where no one would see him. His dragon magic would hide him from people as he flew closer to the town. To a human, he would look like a dark storm cloud rolling through.

He finally made it to the part of town where Faye lived. He flew over her street, finding it empty and quiet. It was late, and he was sure she would be home from work. His dragon remained silent, and he landed, careful not to alarm any of Faye's neighbors. He quickly used his magic to shift his body back to his human form, then waved his hand, conjuring clothes and shoes. He glanced at her home and saw the glow from a soft light on her first floor.

He couldn't shake the feeling that something was bothering her. Something had caused her to experience fear, and his dragon didn't like it. They were to protect her and keep her out of harm's way.

He ran up the steps and hurried down her walkway. He arrived at her door and took a deep breath, trying to calm his nerves. He rang her doorbell and waited, then he came the sound soft footsteps. He waited patiently. She looked through the peephole before the unlocking the door. It slowly opened, revealing his sexy mate.

"Vander," she murmured, a soft smile on her lips.

"Hey." His eyes greedily took her in, noting that she appeared unharmed. She was in her bathrobe, and her dark hair was still damp from her shower. "Can I come in?"

He laughed; she cursed under her breath, fumbling to open the screen door. She pushed it open, and he made his way into her home. He gathered her into his arms, unable to resist taking a taste of her. He covered her mouth with his and kicked the door shut behind him.

Her arms wound their way around his neck and brought him closer to her. He groaned, his tongue dipping inside of her mouth, tasting the mint flavor of her toothpaste.

"I've missed you." Faye said once she broke the kiss.

He rested his forehead against hers, loving the feel of her in his arms. This was just what he and his dragon needed. Holding her in his arms assured his dragon that she was unharmed.

"How did you get here? I didn't hear a car out there."

"I flew." He pulled her over to the couch.

The television was on low, and it was on the local news channel. She brought her legs up and tucked them beneath her, snuggling into him. His beast released a satisfied grumble at the close contact. He could spend the rest of his life like this.

"Wait—you flew?" She leaned back, amazed. "I would love to see your dragon."

"One day." He laid a kiss on her forehead. He couldn't wait for the day, but not yet. His dragon would love to be able to strut in front of her with all of his magnificent scales and power to be seen. Showing his powerful beast would bring them closer. She would be one of few humans who would know that dragons existed. "If you're not afraid of heights, I would love to take you up for a flight."

"Really?" She drew back, excitement lining her face. "Can we go now?"

She moved to jump off the couch, but he caught her hand and tugged her back down.

"Not tonight. I just flew over a thousand miles

to spend time with you," he admitted. He didn't want to come right out and tell her that he could feel her emotions. He had to slowly ease her into the life of a dragon's mate. So, instead of asking her outright why she was experiencing fear, he would see if she would come out and tell him.

"Well, don't I just feel special. You flew all the way to see little ol' me?" She batted her eyelashes at him.

He released a growl and brought her body flush with his.

"You're damn right I did. I've been thinking of nothing but sliding my cock into your tight little pussy," he said.

Her eyes widened with shock, then pure lust at his dirty words. He could tell the same thing had been on her mind. That's how he knew they were meant to spend an eternity together.

"Well, what's stopping you now that you're here?" Her voice grew husky, and she stood from the couch.

He watched, mesmerized, her fingers releasing the tie of her robe. She opened the terry cloth and dropped it to the floor, revealing her naked body to him, his pendant hanging low between her breasts. He released a snarl, sat forward, and snatched his shirt from his body. They would have plenty of time to talk. Right now, his cock was demanding to feel Faye around it.

He released a deep breath, and she kneeled in front of him and brushed his hands aside.

"I'll take care of you tonight," she whispered, her large, dark eyes staring back at him.

He leaned back and lifted his hips to help her; she dragged his jeans and underwear out of the way. He kicked them off to the side. Her small hand wrapped itself around his aching length, caressing him.

He hissed at her lips wrapping around the head. His head fell against the back of the couch.

"Yes," he groaned.

Her mouth was heaven. Vander basked in the sensation of her tongue running along the length of him. His mate's mouth was meant to take him. He bit back a shout, and she stretched her mouth wide and tested herself by taking as much of him as she could. He entwined his fingers in her thick locks.

"Good girl."

Her eyes flew open to meet his. The heat in her beautiful green orbs grew more intense. She paused; her lips remained locked around his shaft. It was one of the most beautiful sights he'd ever been blessed to witness. Vander's heart raced, his breaths coming in short, quick bursts.

Faye's hand slid along him to the base of his cock and squeezed, eliciting another moan from him.

"Fuck. Don't stop," he growled.

Vander wasn't above begging his mate to finish what she had started. She closed her eyes and lowered her head onto him, taking him farther into the depths of her throat. He tightened his grip on her hair and lifted his hips to meet her movements. He gritted his teeth, trying to keep his cock from releasing so soon. He wanted to continue to enjoy all that his mate offered.

But fuck, did he want to release in her mouth. Just the thought of her accepting his seed had his muscles tensing and his balls drawing up tight.

*Not yet.*

He had to hold back a little while longer.

Faye's hand cupped his sac, and all lucid thoughts went out the window.

Yes, his mate was certainly talented and was determined to take his soul.

Little did she know, it already belonged to her.

# CHAPTER NINE

THE SMELL of bacon circulated through the air as Faye hurried to finish breakfast. The shower was running; Vander was finally up. It was mid-morning, and her stomach released an angry growl, demanding to be fed. Thanks to Vander showing up in the wee hours of the morning, she didn't get much sleep, and they'd worked up quite an appetite.

She blew out a nervous breath, sprinkled a little shredded cheese in the eggs, and took the bacon from the oven. She needed to tell him about his friend showing up at her job last night. It still freaked the hell out of her. How could a man just disappear like that? Or, better yet, how did he freeze Teresa in place and take away her memory of it? From what she knew, even shifters didn't have that power. What was that guy?

She grabbed her coffee mug from the counter and took a healthy sip. She sighed and leaned back against the counter, the delicious, caffeinated liquid sliding down her throat.

"What's the sigh for?" Vander's voice broke through her thoughts.

She jumped.

"Huh?" she asked. Turning, she found him in the doorway with just his jeans on. Her eyes were mesmerized by his bare muscular chest and well-defined six-pack.

He stepped into the kitchen and walked toward her.

"After the night we just had, the smell of bacon in the air the next morning and sighing does not go together," he joked and stood in front of her.

She placed her cup back on the counter. He trapped her between the counter and his muscular body. She tipped her head back so she could look at him. His amber eyes always took her breath away. His stare was intense, and he waited for her to speak, the joking put aside.

"What is it?" he asked softly.

"I lost a patient last night." She felt the same

emotions overcome her when they'd pronounced the patient's time of death.

"So sorry to hear," he murmured, concern on his face.

She smiled softly and thought on the events of the evening before.

"Something weird happened last night. After they called the guy's death, I went outside for a breather. It's never easy to lose a patient." She paused, tucking a strand of hair behind her ear.

He patiently waited for her to start again. It felt good to finally get this off her chest. The sheer presence of him comforted her and calmed her nerves. Somehow, she knew this wasn't something she should keep from him. The guy last night gave her the creeps. She might as well spill the beans.

"I was sitting outside, and a friend of yours was there."

"What?" His voice hardened, and his hands tightened on the counter. "Friend? What did he look like? What did he say his name was?"

"Umm, he actually never told me his name. He knew mine, though. It was hard for me to see him since it was dark outside."

"What did he say?" Vander asked, his voice softening, but his eyes darkened, and something dangerous flashed in them.

"For some reason, he knew that you were smitten with me. I didn't tell him anything. I just knew that I was scared—"

"Did he say anything else?" Vander asked, cutting her off.

Her body trembled from the intensity of his stare. Her anxiety climbed higher with her thinking back to last night.

"Yeah, he told me to give you a message. He said for me to tell you to cease your pursuit of him or he would take something of value from you."

Vander growled. Her heart slammed against her chest, and she watched him back away and turn from her. She could see he was torn over something. He combed his hand through his thick hair.

"We need to go," he said. Turning back, he stepped to the stove and cut everything off before taking her arm. He pulled her to her room.

"What's going on?" she cried out.

"Pack a bag, now. You can't stay here."

"Why not? Who was that man?"

"He's no friend of mine. He's an evil dragon shifter who we've been tracking. He recently wiped out an entire village, and we've been hunting him down to exact justice for the survivors of the village."

"What?" she gasped, her hands flying to her mouth. Her heart went out to the unknown people. She couldn't imagine losing everything because of a stranger with a stick up his ass.

"I don't know how he knows about you, but if he does, it will be too dangerous for you to stay here alone."

"Where can I go?" She scrambled for her duffle bag in her closet. She rushed around the room and tossed clothes in the bag. Her thoughts were racing. She didn't know how long she would have to be gone. She would have to tell Jenna and her parents so that people wouldn't think she was missing.

"You'll have to come home with me." Vander leaned against the door.

"To the condo?" She paused at her dresser and looked at him.

"No. My castle in the mountains."

———

*"We're sending a helicopter to you now,"* Feno said through their telepathic link.

Vander paced. Faye packed her final items. He promised that as soon as Faye was safe in the castle, he would hunt Gamair down and tear him apart. Just the thought of what he could have done to Faye sent Vander's dragon into a hot rage. The message was a direct threat, and Vander would be damned if Gamair touched one hair on her head.

When Faye had begun telling her story, he had his suspicions that something was wrong with her; something had brought fear out of her. He had thought she was going to say an animal had snuck up on her or something of that nature, since she had been outside at night. Never in his wildest dreams would he have thought that Gamair would be so bold to as approach her.

But the second she'd announced that his friend had contacted her, he'd immediately reached out to his brother telepathically. They would need to get her out of town immediately. Gamair had to be watching him, and that must be how he'd found her.

"I'm ready." She tossed the straps of the bag over her shoulder.

"Good. My brother is sending transportation to get us," he announced.

They walked into the living room.

"How the hell would he know we needed help?" she asked and hopped around, putting her shoes on.

"We can speak to each other telepathically."

She turned to him, shock plastered across her face.

"I've been speaking to him this entire time. He's dispatched a helicopter to come pick us up."

"Wow." She stared at him with wide eyes.

If this were under different circumstances, he would laugh. But right now, he had to get her to safety.

"So I don't get to fly on a dragon today?" she asked.

"Not today." He chuckled and ushered her out of the condo, taking her duffle bag.

*"Go one street east. There's a field. Chopper should be there in two minutes,"* Feno's voice broke through his thoughts while he waited for her to lock her door.

"Chopper should be here soon," he informed her. He took her hand and pulled her behind him.

The sun was high, a few humans out working in their yards.

"Where's a helicopter going to land?" she asked nervously. She followed him.

"Can we cut through these yards?" he asked.

They quickly made their way down the street.

"Yes. They lead to an empty plot on the other side."

"Perfect," he murmured and led her up one of her neighbors' driveways.

The sound of a helicopter's blades filled the air. They hurried past the garage and found the helicopter descending.

Faye gripped his arm. They waited for the helicopter to touch down. Vander could see Hank, the pilot, give a thumbs-up when it was safe for them to approach.

"I've never been in a helicopter before," Faye announced.

He glanced down and found her eyes wide, locked on the chopper.

"You've flown before, right?" he asked, pulling her toward the oversized aircraft. He was so used to flying that he had to remember that not all humans flew. Flying to him was second nature.

"Well, yeah, but not in a helicopter. Only full-size airplanes. You know, the kind that are big enough for about a hundred or more people," she muttered and gripped his hand tighter.

He could feel her apprehension, and his dragon huffed, wanting to be the one who calmed her down. He brought her under his arm, and they drew closer to the chopper.

"Don't worry. A helicopter is completely safe,

and besides, you're flying with me. Even if the damn thing fell from the sky, I'd catch you."

# CHAPTER TEN

FAYE'S MOUTH dropped open once the castle came into view. She was still reeling from the fact that Vander was a dragon shifter, but now, seeing where he really lived, she was blown away. She glanced over at him and found him staring at her with a small smile on his lips.

"Why are you smiling?" she asked into the headset.

When they were settled into the helicopter, they'd been fitted with headsets in order to communicate, with not just each other, but the pilot.

It had been a smooth and uneventful ride.

Flying over town and witnessing the beautiful landscaped town from above was absolutely breathtaking. Once they'd reached the mountainous region, she'd become captivated by the beauty of nature. She'd never been up this far in the mountains.

Who would have known that at the top of the mountain, there was a real castle built right into the earth?

Vander spoke of his family and described his home to her in great detail to pass the time during the short flight. Just the description of the castle sounded like something that would be found in the movies.

"You're reaction!" he answered and squeezed her hand.

The feel of her hand in his calmed her fears from the flight. She returned the gesture, and the pilot's voice came through the headset, letting them know they were about to descend to the waiting chopper pad.

For some reason, she didn't panic at the thought of being in danger. Deep down, she knew Vander would protect her. His protective and commanding nature led her to believe that this Gamair would not touch her. She fully believed Vander would take the evil dragon out.

She would use this time at his castle to relax. Vander had assured her there would be plenty to do while his brother and friend hunted down the dragon.

"I'm excited yet nervous," she admitted then blew out a shaky breath.

"Nervous about what?" He raised his eyebrow in question.

"Meeting your brother and your friend. What if they don't like me?" She wasn't quite sure where their relationship was going or if they were even *in* one. But what if his brother and friend looked down on her because she wasn't a powerful dragon but only a human?

"If you're with me, then you're with me. That's all that will matter to them."

Their bodies swayed slightly. The chopper finally landed on the pad. The sounds of the blades quieted, and their speed decreased. Vander removed his headset and turned to her. He gently helped her remove her seat belt and headset. The deafening sound of the helicopter died as the door was opened.

Faye turned and found a young man standing with his hand out. She placed hers in his and allowed him to assist her down from the helicopter.

She was in awe of her surroundings. The helipad was built into the mountain. She looked past the helicopter, and nothing but thick clouds that hid the view of the sky from her were in sight. Her ears ached from the altitude. She tried to yawn to relieve the pressure.

"Master Vander, welcome home," the man greeted Vander who stepped out of the chopper and stood next to her.

"Thank you, Claude." Vander nodded. "Grab her bag and place it in my chambers."

"Your chambers?" she asked, her eyes flying to him. They hadn't spoken of sleeping arrangements. That was a bold step, not that she was complaining. After the night they'd just had, she looked forward to many more.

"Yes, sir," Claude responded.

Vander led her away from the chopper.

"Is that a problem?" he asked, looking down at her.

She quickly shook her head, and a massive steel door that was embedded into the mountain wall opened, and out walked an elderly gentleman. He wore a dark suit, reminding her of a butler from earlier times. He met them halfway before stopping in front of them.

"Master Vander and Ms. Adams," he greeted them.

"Farta," Vander replied.

"Welcome to Dragon's Keep, Milady." Farta nodded to Faye.

"Thank you." She took in her surroundings.

"We have a hot meal prepared for you in the breakfast nook," Farta announced and waved them by.

Vander led her to the door through which Farta had exited.

"Excellent. We were in a rush when we left Faye's home, and neither of us were able to eat." Vander led her down a darkened stairwell, where candlelit sconces lined the drab area.

"I can't believe you live in a real castle," she exclaimed, excited to be there. She couldn't wait to explore and learn more about Vander.

"This home has been in my family's possession for centuries. My parents built my brother and me homes as gifts for coming into adulthood."

"Wow," she murmured. The only things her parents were able to give her when she'd turned eighteen was to co-sign for her student loans in order for her to go to college. Her parents were not rich by any means but stressed the importance of furthering her education. She didn't regret it one bit, and soon, those loans would be paid off.

"You'll have time to explore to your heart's content. I can hear the excitement in your voice." Vander chuckled. "Farta, can you assign someone to give her a tour?" Vander asked and came upon a door.

She had lost count of how many flights they had walked down. He opened the door and waved her in.

Her mouth dropped open. She passed through the doorway. She felt as if she were in a fairy tale. This place couldn't be real. She glanced down the hallway and found it to be grand, with priceless artwork on the walls and heirlooms on tables.

"Wow," she breathed. She was at a loss for words as she stood there. She walked over to a painting on the wall that captured her attention.

"Do you like it?" He came to stand next to her.

Farta brushed past them and continued down the hall. "I will assign Dalma to assist Ms. Adams."

"It's beautiful. Dalma?" She tore her eyes off the abstract painting. That green-eyed monster named jealousy reared her nasty head. Who was this female who would be *assigned* to her?

"Dalma is one of the house servants. She's

been with our family for years, and she knows everything about this place, and me."

"She does, does she?" Faye batted her eyes at Vander playfully. On the inside, she was just a little jealous. Who was this woman? How long had she been with Vander? And has she really *been* with him?

"There's nothing to be jealous about." Vander laughed. Grabbing her hand, he pulled her behind him. "She used to be my nanny and decided to stay on with me when I moved into my own home. Hopefully, one day, she'll be the nanny of my children."

"Oh." That was the only response that came to mind. She looked away, and her cheeks grew warm. He was able to read her so well. She glanced back at him and found a certain twinkle in his eye.

"She will love you," he claimed.

They walked through the castle.

She tried to pay attention to where they were going, but there were so many twists and turns, she couldn't keep up. If she were to try to navigate the halls on her own, she was sure she would get lost.

"This place is beautiful, and massive. It would take me days to explore it."

"Thank you. You should be here for a few days, hopefully. Once we find Gamair and destroy him, you will be able to return home. Now, let me feed you."

He tucked her under his arm, and they walked through a set of French doors.

The breakfast nook was a room that was encased in glass. The rounded dome of the ceiling was sheer glass, allowing them to see the sky. She just knew that on a beautiful clear day, with the sun shining, the view of the room would be magnificent.

"Let me help you to your chair." Vander guided her over to the table.

She settled into her seat and watched him go to his chair. For a man his size, his movements were graceful. Memories of their night together came to mind. Every moan and orgasm he pulled from her had her clenching her thighs together.

*Get a grip, girl!* she thought to herself, a small smile graced her lips.

Her curiosity was piqued, and she had at least a dozen questions for him. Yes, they had slept together, but she still didn't know him. She held back on her questioning when a few women entered the room from a door off to the side. Through the door, she caught a glimpse of the kitchen. The women, dressed in traditional maid uniforms, brought out small carts loaded with food toward the table. Her stomach rumbled, the smell of the freshly cooked food filling the air.

"Thank you," she murmured.

They placed their food on the table. Her mouth watered, and she looked down at the plate of omelets, bacon, sausage, hash browns, and toast. Bowls of fresh fruit were set out on the table, along with a few types of juices and coffee. She reached for her fork, and the women directed their carts back to the kitchen.

"What is it?" he asked around his food.

She took a bite out of her omelet and closed her eyes briefly. It was made to perfection. How did they know what she liked in her omelet?

"I'm curious," she began and stopped so that could finish chewing.

"Really?" He chuckled. He reached for his glass and downed half of his orange juice. "What do you want to know?"

"Well, for starters, I noticed that you said this castle had been in your family for centuries, but you said that it was built for you. How old are you?"

Vander paused, then clasped his hands together in front of him. His eyes locked on hers and didn't move. For a split second, she regretted asking the question. Was it rude to ask a shifter their age? A small smile graced his lips, and he picked his fork up again.

"I'm six hundred and ninety-nine years old."

# CHAPTER ELEVEN

VANDER OPENED his bedroom door and ushered Faye into his private domain. His dragon was pleased that she was in love with the castle. When he'd explained how he'd come to live in the castle, he'd left out the real reason his parents had given them to his brother and him. It was so they could prepare their dragon hoard in preparation of them finding their mates.

For years, his dragon had worked on preparing their home for the one day their mate would walk through the doors.

*She is now here.*

"I just can't stop gushing over your home," she exclaimed.

He had allowed her to make a quick phone call to her parents and best friend, using an untraceable phone. He wouldn't want her family worried and getting the Westwend Police Department involved.

"It's absolutely beautiful. I can't believe that I'll be spending a few days in a real castle."

He chuckled and watched her run and dive onto his oversized canopy bed.

A few days?

*How about forever?* a voice whispered to him in the back of his mind.

"You can pretty much have the run of the castle," he announced and closed the door behind him. He walked over and sat on the edge of the bed near her.

She rolled over and turned to him, excitement lining her face.

"I shouldn't be gone but a few days. Farta and the house staff will keep you safe."

"You're leaving me?" The smile disappeared from her face, worry setting in. She pulled herself up and leaned back against the headboard.

He loved the sight of her in his bed, surrounded by his pillows. No other woman had ever had the privilege to visit Dragon's Keep or sleep in his bed.

"Yes, but only for as long as it will take for us to catch Gamair. Between the three of us, we'll end him." His words ended on a growl, the passion bursting forth. Gamair had done unspeakable things, but now, he'd messed with Vander's mate, and for that he would surely die. Vander would not stop until the Death Lord existed no more.

"But what if he comes here while you're gone?"

"Dragon's Keep is one of the safest places in the world. It's protected by magical wards to keep evil away, and nothing will harm you for as long as you are here. Trust me." He grabbed her hand and brought it to his lips. He placed a soft kiss to her knuckles, shifting their hands to entwine their fingers.

"I do, but I'll worry about you. What if you get hurt?"

He stared at her with a raised eyebrow. Had she already forgotten how they'd met? They both burst out laughing. Faye's laugh was musical, and he wanted to continue finding ways to make her laugh, just so he could hear it.

"I'll still worry," she said, wiping the tears from her face.

"There'll be no need for you to worry. I'll be fine," he assured her.

He leaned forward. He couldn't resist getting one last taste of her lips before he left. The kiss was soft and sensual. She immediately opened her mouth to him, allowing his tongue to duel with hers. She wasn't shy in her kiss, allowing her tongue to coax his.

He reached up and cupped her jaw, tilting his head so he could get closer to her. The need to protect what was his grew. He needed this woman, and when he returned, he would make sure she knew that she was his forever.

He pulled back slightly, not wanting to end the kiss. But he knew if they went any further, he'd find himself buried deep within her, and any desire to leave would disappear.

"Promise me, you'll be careful," she whispered with wide eyes. She clenched his shirt tight and hung on to him.

"Believe me, I will return. This time, I have something worth coming home to," he murmured and leaned his forehead against hers.

"And what is that?"

"You."

———

Vander walked around the side of the Westwend General Hospital, where Faye had said Gamair had approached her. His dragon blew out a hot breath at the thought that they could have lost their mate that night. The black dragon was vile and evil-tempered and obsessed with death. He could have done much worse than freeze Faye's friend. He could have killed her easily, along with Faye, but Vander was sure Gamair wanted to terrify Faye, to showcase his powers.

He glanced around, not seeing anyone milling around the smoke hut. He shook his head, not understanding why humans would want to pollute their bodies with the little white death sticks. Humans had enough issues on their own, so why would they smoke? Being a shifter, he was immune to the common human illnesses and diseases.

Vander wasn't sure what he was searching for but figured he'd check around the last spot he knew the evil dragon had been. He would need to use magic to help him.

He was the only one in the parking lot. He reached into his pocket and brought out a small object that would help give him a clue as to where to search for Gamair.

The Orb of Erlo was an ancient artifact that

was given to him by a powerful mage a few centuries ago. By peering through the orb, Vander would be able to see the past. He'd focus his mind on who he was seeking, and the orb would show him what he wanted to see.

Vander brought the orb up to his eye and focused his mind on Gamair. It warmed slightly in his hand. His eyesight, while gazing through the orb, became blurry for a brief moment, then cleared, and the object of his search stood a few feet from where he was now standing. The brief encounter between Faye and Gamair played out in front of him.

He was able to see everything that was exchanged between them but was not able to hear what was said. The Orb didn't allow them to hear, but they could see, feel, and smell anything that passed on that night.

Vander could feel the apprehension and fear that Faye experienced as she sat on the bench. But what gained his attention was the smell. The smell of death and decay, along with the smell of water, surrounded Vander.

He pulled the orb from his eye and knew where he had to go. He released a curse, pocketed the magical lens, and stalked toward his car. He hated that he had to drive while in town. His dragon was far too large to just shift and fly off. A dragon hadn't been seen for hundreds of years. Today would not be the day to show his dragon. It would cause an uproar in town if a dragon was seen flying over Westwend.

He hopped into his dark sedan and figured he'd better contact his brother and Jodos.

*"I know where Gamair has been hiding."* He used their telepathic link to reach out to both of them at same time.

## CHAPTER TWELVE

FAYE WALKED THROUGH THE CASTLE, trying to navigate her way to the kitchen. She had slept surprisingly well in the massive bed alone last night. Vander's bed had to be the most comfortable one she had ever slept in. She almost didn't want to leave the comforts of Vander's pillows and blanket.

She paused in the hallway as the revelation hit her. She had feelings for Vander, and she was pretty sure he had some for her. The thought of Vander going off to fight the evil dragon still worried her, but he'd assured her he would be fine.

"Ms. Adams, good morning," a pleasant voice

greeted her from behind.

She turned and found a smiling older woman. The woman's face was warm and welcoming, her gray hair pulled into a bun on top of her head.

"Hello." Faye returned her smile with one of her own. "You must be Dalma."

"Yes, I am. It is so nice to meet you." Dalma held out her hand.

Faye didn't hesitate in taking it. For someone who had been the nanny of a dragon shifter, who was almost seven hundred years old, she didn't look a day over fifty-five. "Vander has told me so much about you."

"He has?" Her voice ended on a squeak. What could he have possibly told the woman? That they'd met when he was in the hospital, tracked her down, and they'd slept with each other almost immediately?

"I can see the wheels spinning in that mind of yours," Dalma announced. She entwined her arm with Faye's. They slowly walked down the hallway together.

"Don't worry. It has been good. In the shifter world, finding that special one is different than how humans do it. We encourage speedy courtships. Why waste time?"

"We?" Faye's eyes turned to the woman. She

was a shifter, too? Faye wondered what type of shifter this woman was.

"Yes, *we*." Dalma laughed. "And if you were wondering? Yes, I'm a dragon shifter, too. A very old one at that."

"Well, you look good for your age." Faye smiled.

The other woman laughed. Faye's stomach chose that moment to let itself be known. Her cheeks grew warm in embarrassment.

"Why, thank you. Let's feed you. Vander will not forgive me if I don't take good care of you." Dalma chuckled and motioned for Faye to follow her.

"I didn't realize how hungry I was," Faye admitted.

They walked into the kitchen. A few staff members were bustling around. A man dressed in a white chef's jacket turned from the oven with a loaf of bread, fresh from the oven, in his hand. He placed it on the counter and walked over to them.

"Faye, this is Eduardo. He's the head chef here at Dragon's Keep."

"Buenos días," he greeted and extended his hand.

"It's an honor to meet you, Chef. The food that

comes out of this kitchen is amazing." Faye took the chef's hand in a firm shake.

Her stomach rumbled again, and they all laughed.

"I have a plate in the warmer just for you. Since you are the only guest as of now, we can set you up in the dining room or—"

"Can I just eat in here?" She looked around at the massive-sized kitchen. Any cook worth their salt would salivate over this beautiful, industrialized room.

"You sure can. You can sit over here." Eduardo motioned to the bar stools that sat alongside the countertops. He snapped his fingers and rattled off words in Spanish.

One of the women in the kitchen grabbed the plate and brought it over to Faye.

"Well, when you're done visiting and eating, just call me and we can take you on your first tour of the castle." Dalma patted her on her shoulder.

"Yes, ma'am." Faye glanced down at her plate. Her mouth watered at the sight of the delicious food. She would have to find some time to work out. Otherwise, she'd gain twenty pounds in the few days she would be staying here.

She dug into the food and groaned. It was

everything that she could have imagined. How would she be able to leave this place in a few days once Vander had defeated Gamair?

———

"What's down that hallway?" Faye peered down a hall that was blocked off with a table filled with potted plants.

Dalma was a wonderful tour guide. She was chatty and knew the history of the home well. They had walked through the castle for a few hours, and Faye had enjoyed Dalma's company immensely. She had all the good stories of Vander growing up. Faye couldn't remember the last time that she had laughed so hard.

But something drew her to that particular hall. A stainless-steel door with a bolt on it at stood the end of the hallway. What could be so important that it would require protection behind a door such as that?

Vander's words echoed in her head from the day he'd left. *'You can pretty much have the run of the castle.'*

Was there something he didn't want her to see? What could he be hiding?

"Oh, that hallway? Well, Vander has some

private things that he likes to keep locked away." Dalma waved her hand and grabbed on to Faye's arm. "You know how boys are about their toys."

Faye offered a small smile. Dalma pulled her in the opposite direction of the secret room. Something was amiss. Dalma was keeping a secret.

*Vander's secret.*

"Boys will be boys," Faye murmured.

"Don't worry, dear. I'm sure he will show you. Hopefully, he'll be returning soon." Dalma patted her on the hand. She must have seen the suspicion on Faye's face.

Faye felt slightly better, and they walked in the opposite direction.

"Have you spoken to him?" Faye asked. Since he'd left, there hadn't been any communication between the two of them. She didn't want to be a distraction to him and was sure that when he was able, he would contact her.

There was much for her to do, but it still didn't keep her from worrying about Vander. Last night, she had gone swimming in the beautiful Olympic-sized indoor pool, then relaxed in the sauna, before venturing around the castle and into the library. It had been a while since Faye had had time to just relax and read a book. She'd fallen asleep, reading a romance novel, that led her to have a steamy dream that included Vander.

"No, I haven't, my dear. When the boys go on missions such as these, it's best to leave them alone and wait for word. They look out for each other. I'm sure everything is just fine."

# CHAPTER THIRTEEN

VANDER DIRECTED his dragon to fly lower beneath the clouds. Thanks to the Orb of Erlo, Vander was able to figure out where Gamair could be hiding. The smell of death, decay, and water, could only mean one thing.

*The Wetlands.*

Darkness was approaching, and he knew that if Gamair were near, he would show himself soon. Vander was familiar with the evil dragon's actions. Gamair loved to hunt and attack at night.

*"Any signs of him?"* Jodos asked, using their telepathic link.

*"No, nothing,"* he replied.

The swampy, bug-infested waters were the perfect place for Gamair to hide out. Vander's dragon pumped his wings harder, gaining more speed. They had to hurry so they could put an end to this. Gamair needed to die before he harmed other people.

*"I found him."* Feno's voice broke through. *"Lock on to my location and get your asses here."*

Vander's dragon located Feno's, who was only a few miles away. Vander directed his dragon to turn into the direction of his brother. This time, the three of them would work together to capture and destroy the black dragon. He pushed his dragon harder, anticipation for the coming battle mounting. He needed to keep Faye safe. That was his top priority. Once they took out Gamair, he could focus on mating with her, and living forever with the one woman who was made just for him.

He flew higher, wanting to make sure he was able to get the black dragon into his line of sight. Feno's dragon came into his vision, and Jodos' dragon suddenly appeared, flying alongside his brother as the black dragon led them on a chase.

*"Vander, get your pansy ass over here,"* Feno commanded.

*"Old man, you need to get your eyes checked. I'm right above you,"* Vander retorted.

Gamair let loose a dragon roar that echoed through the air. He finally detected that he was not the only dragon in the sky. Vander would have to be more careful tonight. There would not be a repeat of before, which had landed him in the Westwend Hospital. Not this time. Vander would be ready.

*"He's going toward land."* Feno's voice broke through.

*"Good. I didn't feel like going for a swim,"* Vander replied. His dragon hated water. It wasn't that he wouldn't be able to swim in his dragon form, it was just that dragons were a fire species who preferred to stay in the air, raining fire down on their enemies, not frolicking in the muddy waters of the Wetlands.

They moved into a triad formation, with Feno in the lead. His brother dove down, crashing his massive body onto the dark dragon. Their bodies tumbled through the air, with Feno landing on top of the black dragon, pushing him toward the ground.

Jodos and Vander followed, tucking their wings to their sides, gaining speed and piercing the sky, jetting through the air toward the ground.

*"Feno, pull up,"* Vander shouted.

His brother was heading for the ground at

record speed, and unless he wanted to end up in the hospital like Vander had, he needed to let the dragon go before they approached barren land. Feno's wings spread out, slowing his descent through the air. The black dragon slammed into the ground. Each of their dragons made a safe landing. Staying in dragon form, they quickly made their way to the fallen dragon.

*"Is he dead?"* Jodos asked.

They approached the dragon's side.

*"Doubt it,"* Feno replied.

Vander stared at the fallen creature. He wasn't sure why, but alarms went off in the back of his mind. The massive beast lay, unmoving, on the ground. Vander's dragon growled, ready to blow out his flames onto their captive, but the human in Vander knew something was wrong.

*"Something's different,"* Vander announced.

*"What the hell do you mean?"* Jodos groaned. *"We've chased this dragon for months, and now you say something's wrong?"*

*"We've been chasing Gamair, the Death Lord,"* Vander said. His eyes narrowed on the black dragon before them. *"But this isn't Gamair."*

*"What?"* Feno growled who moved in closer to the black one.

A bright light glowed from the dragon which began to shift. They all watched the human form appear before them.

It was not Gamair.

Vander pulled back on his dragon and shifted back to his human form. He needed to see for himself and confirm that it was not Gamair. His brother and Jodos followed suit. They cautiously approached the fallen figure, and manic laughter filled the air. Vander's eyes flew to Feno's, and they reached the figure that lay in the high grass.

No, this was definitely not Gamair.

Vander let loose a curse and stood over the deranged man.

"Who the hell are you?" Vander growled, his chest rising and falling feverishly, his anger mounting. They'd wasted time. Where the hell was Gamair?

"Tyson Nautilus." The man released a cynical chuckle. "Gamair was right. He knew you would follow me. Our dragons are very similar, and we've been mistaken for each other before."

"Oh, really?" Feno grabbed Tyson by his neck and dragged him up to a standing position. After shifting from dragon to their human forms, it left them naked. Neither of them were bothered by their nakedness, as it was part of a shifter's life. "Since your dragons look so similar, what if we just put an end to you like we plan to do with him?"

"Sounds like a plan to me," Jodos growled.

"Where is he?" Vander demanded and stood in front of Tyson. They could do with him what they liked, after he got information out of him.

"You've hunted him down, but now it is he who is the hunter." Tyson chuckled again.

Vander narrowed his eyes on the piece of shit of an excuse of a dragon shifter. The laughter was getting on Vander's last nerve. They could end him right here, and no one would know. It was tempting, but right now, they had to find Gamair. This Tyson character wasn't worth expelling the energy it would take to kill him.

"Let me end him now," Jodos growled, moving closer to him.

Vander held up a hand, the alarms at the back of his mind continuing to go off. His imagination took off as he thought. Why would Gamair want them to follow a decoy? Where the hell was the Dragon Lord?

*'He said to tell you to cease your pursuit of him, or he will take something of value from you.'* Faye's words echoed in his mind.

It hit him.

Faye.

Gamair was going after his mate.

"Faye. He's going after her," Vander announced and looked to Feno and Jodos.

"You sure?" Feno asked, his sharp eyes cutting to Vander.

"I'm positive. I should have known." Vander cursed himself for falling for the ruse. He should have ensured Faye was better protected. The wards of the castle had been there for centuries, but he should have had them reinforced.

"Go!" Feno commanded.

Vander didn't have to be told twice. He turned and strode away. He had to get to Dragon's Keep, and fast!

"You're too late!" Tyson shouted from behind him.

A yelp filled the air, and Vander turned to see the shifter's body collapse to the ground at his brother's feet.

"Hurry. We'll be right behind you, as soon as we take care of this idiot," Jodos insisted.

Vander nodded and spun back, calling forth his dragon. They would have to be quick. There was no telling if Gamair had made it to Faye. As Vander's dragon took off into the air, he said a prayer, hoping they weren't too late. His dragon sensed the urgency and cut through the air swiftly. He had promised Faye he would keep her safe, and dammit, he would.

# CHAPTER FOURTEEN

"LET'S go out to the gardens. We can have lunch there," Dalma announced as she burst through the library doors.

Faye had become quite smitten with the castle's library. The grand room housed two floors full of books that waited for her to discover them all. The smell of leather and cedarwood filled the air and helped her relax. Since discovering the library, she had found a comfortable leather chaise located near a window with a magnificent view. Faye loved coming to sit by the window so she could look out into the sky.

It offered a direct view of the cloud-streaked sky. Some days, the clouds floated by, blocking her view of the sun when it rose. On a clear day, Faye could glance down at the world below them.

"I can go outside?" Faye asked, surprised.

"But of course! You're not a prisoner. You may go where you please. You just cannot leave the grounds."

"Well, then, lead the way," she said, scrambling off the chaise. She placed her bookmark in the book she was reading. She wasn't an animal that would bend the tip of the page. She was a civilized human being who used a bookmark, she thought, and laid it on the chaise. She would return later to finish it.

"The garden is full of such rich history of the Kelmyar Clan," Dalma told her.

They walked along the stone path. The luxurious gardens were plush and green, with high bushes.

"Wow, is this a maze?" Faye took it all in. The beauty of the location took her breath away. A slight breeze blew her hair into her face. She brushed the strands away and glanced at the clear blue sky. It had taken her a few days to get used to the mountain air, but she loved it now. The crisp air was soothing to her while they walked.

"No, not a maze." Dalma giggled. "It was

designed to entertain. Let me show you something special."

They turned the corner, and there, in a small clearing, was a beautiful bronze statue of a massive dragon.

"Oh, my. It's beautiful," Faye breathed and walked closer to it. The dragon was posed in a defiant manner. The eyes were narrowed, as if it was hunting its prey.

"This is Vander and Feno's father," Dalma announced, as if she were introducing Faye to him in real life.

Faye stepped closer to the statue, and her eyes fell to the nameplate that was at the base of it.

*Tordet Kelmyar, The Dragon Lord.*

"He looks so fierce," Faye noted and admired the oversized statue.

"Well, he would have to be, with those two boys of his. Vander and Feno were just a handful growing up." Dalma laughed and shook her head. "He's the protector of the dragon shifters. He is *the* Dragon Lord."

"Wow," Faye murmured. Living in Westwend, she was used to the paranormal world. Vampires, shifters, and witches were commonly known throughout the community. But to know that dragons did exist, and she was in love with one—

She paused. *In love?* With Vander? She dug down deep and knew it was true.

"Come. Let's move on to the next." Dalma gently guided her by the arm.

They continued to walk. Dalma was the perfect guide, giving her the history behind the Kelmyar Clan and the reasoning behind them never showing themselves.

"So, basically, they just want to live their lives in peace and protect their kind," Faye confirmed.

They came to the next statue.

"Yes. The dragon shifters are one of the most powerful of the paranormal world, and it's best for them to stay hidden."

"Who is that?" Faye gasped.

They came upon a fierce dragon who appeared to be ready for battle. The fierceness of the eyes, the display of the sharp talons, had her breath catching in her throat. She could almost feel the power radiating off it as she stared at the copper statue.

"Go ahead. Look at the nameplate." Dalma gave her a nudge and a smile.

Faye stepped up to it and looked down at the nameplate.

*Vander Kelmyar, The Warrior.*

It was a depiction of her dragon.

*Her* warrior dragon, who was currently off ensuring she was protected by taking out the threat of an evil dragon.

She reached out a hand and laid it on Vander's dragon. She allowed her fingers to trace along the smooth metal of his arm and down to the talons, and stared up in awe at the massive statue.

She closed her eyes and sent up a short prayer, knowing that wherever he may be, he was probably in danger, trying to keep her safe. But, looking at the fierceness of the dragon in front of her, she thought it was the evil dragon who should be worried.

"He really cares for you." Dalma's soft voice broke through her thoughts, and she came to stand next to her.

"And I, him," she murmured, opening her eyes. She wished she could tell him how she felt at the moment but knew she would have to wait. Their relationship was a whirlwind and blowing by too fast. Her mind and heart were in the middle of a battle. Her mind screamed that this was not normal and that they should take their time getting to know each other, while her heart was steadfast in its belief.

*You love who you love.*

Even though she was in the midst of an

internal battle, something whispered to her to hold on tight. He was *the* one for her. She slowly backed up from the statue, unable to take her eyes off Vander's dragon. She just knew it would be magnificent in person, and she couldn't wait for him to return.

"Now, let's move on. We have more of the family to show you," Dalma said with a twinkle in her eye.

"These statues are beautiful, and I'm sure they don't do their dragons justice," Faye replied with a laugh. She entwined her arm with the older woman's, thrilled to be able to learn more about Vander's family.

"They don't. I'm sure Vander has planned to have you meet—"

Her words were cut off by the sounds of a deafening roar from above. Faye covered her ears and looked up. A shadow passed overhead. She froze in place, her eyes locked on those of a black dragon. It was larger than she would have ever expected. It was easily longer than a few hundred feet. Her mouth flapped open, and she watched it fly away. She didn't need to be told who the dragon was.

*Gamair.*

"Oh, no!" Dalma gasped, pulling on Faye's

arm. "We've got to go!"

Faye didn't hesitate. She turned and ran behind the older woman. For the woman to be the age she admitted to, she sure could sprint. Faye glanced behind her and found the black dragon headed straight for them. She picked up her speed, wishing she had kept up the workout she had abandoned so long ago.

Darkness surrounded them. The dragon reached them, blocking the sun with his massive form. She would not be able to outrun a dragon.

"Dalma!" she screamed out.

The rough talons of the dragon grabbed her by the waist, plucking her from the ground. She fought to release herself but was no match for the dragon's tight grip. He carried her off.

"Faye!" Dalma's voice drew faint as the dragon flew away.

She looked down at how far they were from the ground. He spirited her away from the castle. She let loose a scream and scrambled to hold on to the leg of the dragon for dear life. She wouldn't survive if he decided to let her go.

A distant roar filled the air. Faye glanced back down at the castle and saw a smaller dragon making its way toward them.

*Dalma.*

Hope filled her chest that Dalma's dragon would be able to save her. The smaller dragon was swiftly heading toward them, but Faye's hope was soon doused. Gamair's chest rumbled; he discovered they were being followed. A bright beam of light shot from the black dragon.

Faye screamed and watched the energy ball slam into Dalma's dragon.

"Dalma!" she screamed and watched, horrified.

The smaller dragon fell from the sky, disappearing through the clouds. Faye tightened her grip on the dragon's leg, tears clouding her vision. She didn't want to think of what could have happened to the sweet dragon shifter. She prayed Dalma would survive.

A new fear entered her chest. If Gamair was here, where was Vander?

# CHAPTER FIFTEEN

"WHERE IS SHE?" Vander roared. He burst through the doors of the castle. He instantly sensed Faye was gone. His dragon knew it. It sensed the loss the moment they had landed.

"It was the Death Lord, sir," Farta announced and stalked toward Vander.

"How did he break through the wards of the property?" Vander growled.

"We don't know," Farta admitted. He followed behind Vander. "We have been working at repairing the wards, sir."

Vander let loose a roar of angst and pain that shook the floors. His mate had been taken from their home. Somewhere that was to be a sanctuary for her, and she was just snatched away. Plucked from the grounds that were to protect her from evil. He stood there, breathing hard. His beast wanted to break free and fly off in search of their mate.

"How did he get her?" he demanded and walked down the hall, Farta trailing behind him. The castle was in an unusual uproar. "What is going on?" he asked, suddenly noting the frantic nature of a few servants running up the stairs to the upper level of the castle.

"It's Dalma, sir," Farta informed him softly.

Vander stood at the bottom of the stairs. The pit of his stomach gave way at the tone of Farta's voice.

"What's wrong with Dalma?" he asked, turning to his head servant.

"She was with Ms. Adams when Gamair came. They were out in the gardens to allow Ms. Adams some fresh air, and you know Dalma, sir. She was introducing her to the family statues."

Vander glanced up at the stairs of the castle. He knew Dalma loved his family so and had fallen in love with Faye immediately, just as he had. He climbed the stairs two at a time. Before going after Gamair, he needed to check on the woman who was like a second mother to him.

He quickly made his way to her suite and watched a few females rush into her room. He stood at the door, unsure of what he would find once he entered. Knowing Dalma as well as he did, he knew that if Gamair had taken Faye in her presence, she would have shifted and gone after them.

He pushed the door open and paused. She came into view. She lay still on the bed, and one of the females adjusted the pillows beneath her head. The other fussed over the blankets.

A growl resonated deep in his chest at the sight of Dalma. Bruises covered her body, and he knew instantly what had happened.

Flashes of his fall came to mind, and he knew she'd experienced the same as he had when Gamair had hit him with his energy.

He forced himself to go into the room. The servants bowed their heads and moved to the corner. He approached Dalma's bed. Her chest rose in a slow, steady rhythm, showing that she was in a deep healing sleep. Her dragon would repair all the damage from her fall. He sat on the edge of the bed and brushed a few of her graying strands of hair from her face.

He leaned forward and placed a kiss to the middle of her forehead.

"He will pay for what he has done to you," Vander vowed. He knew she wouldn't hear him, but it was something he had to put out in the universe.

Gamair may have signed his death warrant before for attacking the villagers and going after his mate. But now, the fiery pits of Hell would never do. He would send the Death Lord to the place beneath Hell.

"How is she?" Feno's low growl broke through the silent air.

"She's in a healing stasis," Vander announced, looking up at the door.

His brother's fierce gaze met his, and his face displayed the same emotion that rumbled deep within his chest.

*Rage.*

They would avenge the villagers and Dalma and take back his mate.

"From what Farta said, he has a couple of hours on us," Feno disclosed.

Vander stood and made his way to the door. They stood outside the door to allow the servants to tend to Dalma.

"He has her," Vander growled. His dragon slammed against his chest, demanding to be let out again. It was ready to seek revenge against the

Death Lord. The warrior in him knew they would fight to the death to protect Faye.

"We will find them and bring her back," Feno assured him.

"If he's harmed one hair on her head—" Vander stopped and looked away. He couldn't verbalize it. If Faye were harmed, he would go crazy. His dragon would lose his mind.

"We'll get your back, little brother. Nothing will happen to your mate. Gamair is playing a sick game."

"I will end the sick fuck's game." Vander stalked toward the stairs.

"We need to come up with a plan. We can't just rush off. He's going to expect us to show up." Feno stormed up behind Vander.

"Well, let me not disappoint him," Vander snapped.

They reached the bottom of the stairs.

"Stop!" Feno commanded. Grabbing him by the arm, he swung him around to face him.

Vander turned a cold eye to his brother. Feno could never begin to understand what he was going through. This was his mate they were talking about. She was in the hands of their enemy. Someone who was devious, pure evil, and wouldn't give two fucks about killing a human.

"Don't push me away. I'm on your side. But if we're to get your mate back, we must work together. A plan must be developed so that we don't mess this up. We're going to have one chance to get her back."

"I don't give a damn what happens to me. It's Faye who I care about," he snapped. His dragon was ready to go off to bring their mate home. There was so much they had yet to share with her. Little did she know, this castle was hers.

"And that is exactly why I said we need a plan! I refuse to lose my only brother. We do this my way, and only my way. I'm the eldest, and I will have you locked up."

"You wouldn't dare," Vander growled, his eyes narrowed on his brother.

Feno had never threatened him before. His brother had lost his mind if he thought Vander would sit by and allow him to rescue Faye without him.

"To save my hotheaded little brother from running blindly into battle, I would." Feno crossed his arms in front of his massive chest. He cocked an eyebrow and waited for Vander's answer.

Vander paused and glared at his brother. Going by Feno's expression, he would.

"And I'd help him." Jodos' voice appeared behind him.

He glanced at his friend as he came and stood next to Feno.

*Two against one.*

Vander released a sigh and ran a shaky hand across his face. He refused to fight with them. By the looks of them, Vander would lose.

"What do you suggest we do?"

# CHAPTER SIXTEEN

FAYE RELEASED a scream as her body fell through the air. She looked down at the murky water rushing up to greet her. She closed her eyes and held her breath, and she hit the water, hard. She had to beat down the panic that rose in her chest. Her arms flailed around, and her body began its ascent to the top of the water. She kicked her legs to guide her to the surface.

She gasped and broke through the surface, her lungs burning from being deprived of air. She tread water and frantically looked around. She tried to take deep breaths and avoid taking in the nasty water. The dragon flew overhead and released a deafening roar.

*Where the hell are we?*

She desperately searched for land. She wasn't the best swimmer and knew she would tire soon. She sensed a presence quietly drifting behind her so turned. She held in a scream. A large decaying animal carcass floated past her. The dragon flew overhead again. She slipped beneath the water's surface and swam away, trying to put as much distance as she could between her and the dead animal.

She couldn't tell what it was, and somehow, she knew it had met the same fate as she would. She broke the surface, unable to hold her breath any longer. The smell in the air was nauseating. The aroma of death surrounded her, and she had to force the contents of her stomach back down that were trying to escape. She glanced to her right and finally saw land.

She took off into the disgusting water, keeping her attention on the land. She didn't want to know what else was in there with her and pushed herself until she was finally able to put her feet on solid ground. Her feet carried her further until she reached the base of a tree. Her body slammed into the ground as she sat hard.

She leaned her back against the tree, her breaths coming rapidly. She glanced into the sky and found no signs of her captor. Fear gripped her, almost paralyzing her, but she knew she couldn't stay here. He would come for her.

She shoved off the ground and stood on shaky legs. Her drenched clothes made it almost impossible for her to run, but she had to try. She didn't know where she was going, but she moved as fast as her water-soaked clothes would allow. She headed toward a line of trees that were up ahead. She glanced behind her and still didn't see the dragon. Faye sent up a prayer that he would think she had drowned and wouldn't come for her.

She entered the brush of trees and hid behind a thick trunk, trying to control her breathing. She brushed the wet hair from her forehead with a shaky hand, then placed it against her chest, landing on something hard beneath her shirt.

*Vander's dragon eye.*

She pulled it from beneath her drenched shirt and rubbed it between her fingers. The action encouraged a calmness to spread throughout her body. It was as if Vander himself was there to calm her down. She bit back a sob, looking around at her surroundings.

She knew he would come for her. Her dragon warrior would not let her down. She just had to survive until he reached her.

"Vander," she whispered and closed her eyes. She knew it was silly, but she wished she could reach out to him. To speak to him. To hear his voice. She had heard plenty of times of paranormals being able to speak to each other, and this was one time she wished she was of the paranormal world. She prayed that his pendant would allow him to hear her plea for help.

"No use in calling on your dragon lover," a chilling voice announced.

Her eyes flew open, and there he stood. She would recognize his figure anywhere.

"He can't hear you."

Gamair.

"Just let me go," she demanded, trying to ensure that her voice didn't shake. She tried as best as she could to appear brave. "If you let me go now, Vander will let you live."

"He'll let me live? Silly human. Your boyfriend is no match for me. I warned him, that if he did not cease his pursuit of me, that he would lose something of value to him. So, you can thank him for putting revenge for that ratchet farming village over your life."

"He's only doing what is right," she goaded him. She knew that this man, this shifter, was dangerous. She was proud that

Vander would hunt this being to avenge the innocent. She stood tall as she stared him in the eye.

"Your false sense of bravery is almost believable, even downright cute." He chuckled and advanced on her.

She peered around and knew she wouldn't be able to outrun a shifter.

"Too bad no one will be here to save you."

A shiver ran down her spine. He moved closer. Just one look into his eyes, and she knew he was sick in the head. *Deranged*.

"I'm warning you," she stammered and stepped away from the tree, trying to back up.

"You're in no position to threaten me," he growled and marched toward her.

*Fuck this*, she thought and took off, running deeper into the woods. His laughter filled the air behind her, and she pumped her arms and pushed herself.

A force hit her from behind, ripping a scream from her. She fell. Her body slid across the hard ground before drawing to a stop. She attempted to roll to her side and found her body unable to do the maneuver. She willed her arms to move, but it was like invisible ropes kept her arms bound to her sides.

"No," she moaned, fighting with all her might, but her body wouldn't budge.

"Tsk...tsk..." Gamair's voice drew closer behind her.

A lone tear made its way down her cheek as she lay there, vulnerable to him.

"Vander," she whispered, desperately praying he would come for her. He had to. He'd promised he would always protect her.

"I told you, your boyfriend isn't here to help you."

———

*"Vander..."*

The faint sound of Faye's voice filled Vander's head. His pendant! Excitement filled his chest; he realized she still wore the pendant he'd given her. It would allow him to track her.

*"I know where she is,"* he informed Feno and Jodos through their mental link. His dragon let loose a huff, and he turned in the direction of the last signal the pendant had given off.

The damn Wetlands.

He should have known Gamair would go there. He just prayed they weren't too late. He knew what type of carnage was waiting in the

Wetlands. Gamair's dragon loved to feast on rotten flesh that decayed in the murky waters there. His dragon pushed itself faster at the image of Faye, floating in the waters with the decaying animals, coming to mind.

*"Where?"* Feno's deep voice broke through his thoughts.

*"The Wetlands,"* Vander answered.

*"You really think he would take her there?"* Jodos asked.

*"I can sense her through my pendant."*

Curses filled his head. Both Feno and Jodos knew that a dragon's pendant wouldn't lead them astray.

*"Is she still alive?"* Feno asked gently.

*"Yes, I heard her voice,"* he growled, knowing it was more than just her voice he'd heard. He'd heard and sensed the fear inside her. She was frightened, panicking, and alone.

*"We stick together,"* Feno reminded them. *"No hero bullshit. We stand against him together."*

Vander pushed his dragon faster, his wings slicing through the air, eating up the distance. His dragon was in battle mode, and they closed in on Faye's location. If one hair was harmed on her head, he would tear Gamair limb from limb.

The smell of stale water and rotting flesh filled

his nostrils, denoting they were close to the Wetlands. Vander scanned the waters as soon as they came into sight, instantly looking for Faye.

The three dragons stayed in a triangular formation flying over the waters. Vander glanced toward the sun and saw it was making its descent. They would need to hurry. Once nighttime fell, it would make it harder for them to find her. The Wetlands stretched on for miles, and in the dark, there was no telling what creatures would be on the hunt.

*"Any sign of her?"* Jodos asked.

*"No,"* Vander growled. There wasn't even a sign of Gamair. It was hard to hide a dragon that was larger than the size of a football field.

*"A couple miles ahead, there's a small mountainous region. I bet he's holed up there,"* Feno said.

*"It's worth a shot,"* Vander replied, falling in line behind his brother, leading the way.

## CHAPTER SEVENTEEN

THE MOUNTAINOUS REGION that Feno spoke of came into view, and Vander wasn't sure he would really call it a mountain region. More like hills and valleys. It was nothing like the massive mountain his castle sat on.

*"I'm going to shift and land. He'll hear us coming if we stay in dragon form,"* Vander announced. If they were to rescue Faye, the only way he would be able to find her in the hills would be in human form. She had yet to see him in his dragon form, and he wouldn't want to scare her off.

*"Jodos, shift with him. I'll stay in my dragon form and patrol the air,"* Feno instructed.

*"Will do,"* Jodos replied.

They circled around the land.

Vander's dragon descended toward land. He shifted midair, dropping a few hundred yards to the ground. He stood and glanced down at his naked self. With a wave of his hand, he was fully clothed with jeans, a T-shirt, and hiking boots.

"Which way first?" Jodos asked, coming to stand next to Vander.

He turned to his longtime friend and found him dressed similarly. He glanced around but didn't see much. The land was not plush and thriving as it probably should have been.

The trees were dying. Where there should have been rows of vibrant greenery, were rows of trees, spotted with brown leaves. They looked like naked skeletons and were past saving. The land was sick, and it wouldn't survive long. Vander knew the source of the destruction of the land.

*Gamair.*

"Let's go up. There are a lot of hiding places in this area." Vander closed his eyes and tried to place Faye. He sensed she was near.

They began the hike up the hills, through the dense woods. No words were needed in their search for Faye. Vander tried to focus on her and the pendant. He just needed her to call on it again as she had before.

If only he would have explained the pendant to her. It was a way to link a human mate to their dragon shifter; a way to communicate between mates. The pendant would show any other dragon shifter who the human belonged to. But, more importantly, it acted as a beacon to allow him to find her.

As soon as they found her and got her to safety, he would lay it all on the line and tell her she was his mate.

"Come on, Faye, speak to me," he murmured.

They came to a clearing.

"Over there." Jodos pointed.

Vander's eyes turned to where his friend indicated, and he saw a little cave. He doubted that Gamair would hide in such a small area, but it was worth a shot.

His heart sped up with the thought that she would be stashed in the cave opening, cold and alone. He jogged over to the opening and peered inside.

———

Faye grimaced and tried to move her arm again. Gamair had taken her immobile body and stashed her inside a dark, drafty cave. Her clothes, hardening as they dried on her, itched her skin and just about drove her insane. Her hand rested a couple of millimeters from where her leg itched. She let loose a curse.

It still wouldn't budge.

*What type of magic is this?* she groaned to herself. *Doesn't it wear off?*

She grunted, her head falling back against the rock wall in defeat. She swore the minute she was free, no one would stop her from taking a shower and scrubbing the muck off. She just prayed she lived long enough to get that shower. She glanced around the empty cave and could see the sunlight fading.

Gamair had left her alone, and she hoped Vander would kick his ass and free her. She had faith in her dragon warrior. He would come for her. Her head fell forward, and her chin rested on her chest. The pendant beneath her shirt lay beneath her chin.

"Vander," she whispered, rubbing her chin on the hidden pendant. Warmth radiated from beneath her shirt and against her chin. Again, calmness came over her. She just knew everything would be all right.

Vander was near.

She gasped at a shadow at the opening of the

cave. She looked up, and all hope was dashed. Gamair strode into the musty cavern toward her. Her heart sped up at his narrowed look. Was this how she would meet her end? Her entire life seemed to flash before her eyes. Snippets of her life raced in front of her as he approached her.

"Change of plans," he snapped, grabbing her by her arm.

Immediately, she felt the release of her limbs. She breathed a sigh of relief at regaining control of her body. He dragged her to her feet.

"What's going on?" she squealed.

He pulled her behind him.

"Your boyfriend and his band of warriors are too close," he announced.

They left the hideaway. She glanced behind them, and he led her up, higher into the wooded hill.

She knew Vander would come for her.

He didn't let her down.

She grunted; her foot hit a stone hidden in the dirt, and she almost crashed to the ground. Gamair growled and snatched her arm. She yelped at the sharp tug.

"You're going to pull my arm out of the socket," she snapped, trying to wrench her arm back.

"That's going to be the least of your worries,"

he growled. He tugged harder and continued to rush up the path.

She couldn't let him get to the top of the hill. She was sure if he shifted and took off with her, she would never see Vander again. She glanced behind her into the woods and knew what she would have to do.

Scream.

"Vander!" She screamed as loud as her lungs would allow her to. Her voice echoed through the air.

"Bitch!" Gamair bit out.

Swinging his arm at her, he caught her on the side of her face. She tumbled back, falling on her ass. Her cheek stung from the slap. She turned and found him glaring down at her. He approached her. She grinned through the pain, sure that Vander heard her.

If Gamair was going to take her, she would have to put up a fight, long enough for Vander to reach her.

Her smile faded. The ground rumbled beneath her. She glanced around, thinking it would open up and swallow her, but everything around her trembled. She found Gamair staring at the sky.

"See what you've done?" He sneered at her. "Now I must kill your mate in front of you." He took off running up the path and disappeared into the woods.

Through the trees she saw a massive shadow flying overhead.

*My mate?*

Is that why Vander was going above and beyond for a woman he'd just met? Was she his mate?

"Vander," she whispered, her heart pounding. She'd never seen his dragon but knew deep down it was him.

The roar of a dragon filled the air, the ground rumbling again.

She scrambled to her feet and almost fell again. The ground shook beneath her. She regained her footing and took off running in the direction that Gamair had disappeared. A second dragon's roar filled the air. This one's was so powerful, the wind blew the trees back and knocked her back a few steps. She had to be close, so she pushed forward, keeping her eyes on the sky.

The trees finally thinned out, and she came to a halt at the edge of the woods. At the top of the hill was a large clearing that held two dragons circling each other. Her eyes widened, taking in the black dragon, but it was the newcomer that held her attention. He looked just like his statue, but even more fierce, much larger, and more dangerous.

A deafening screech grabbed her attention. The black dragon attacked Vander. With nowhere else to go, she slid behind a wide tree, her heart all but jumping in her throat.

The battle began.

## CHAPTER EIGHTEEN

THE SOUND of Faye's scream echoed in the back of his mind. He knew he had been close to her from her voice whispering in his head, but once he heard his name screamed, his dragon burst free. It was no longer willing to sit back. The shifting in the middle of woods wreaked havoc on the already dying forest. His dragon was too large for the area, but it didn't matter. Faye was in danger.

He sensed her close by and circled Gamair. His dragon was in pure beast mode. Gamair thought he was impossible to defeat. The Death Lord assumed he was too powerful for Vander, but that was where the black dragon was wrong. He had never fought Vander, The Warrior, who was protecting his mate.

Even Vander couldn't control his beast this time. Gamair came in for the attack, but Vander's dragon was in control and able to bat him off, twisting around and going for Gamair's neck. He had to stay on the Death Lord and not let him use his energy. Vander's teeth sank into the dragon, and Gamair bellowed out in pain. The dragon kicked him off, and Vander lost his grip on him.

Gamair took advantage of the kick and advanced again, trying to knock Vander down, but Vander recovered quickly. With a quick, deep breath, he blew out his scorching flames from his mouth.

Gamair let loose a scream. The flames danced along his scales. He tried to turn and run, pumping his wings as if to take off.

He was not getting in the air. If he did, there was no telling where this battle would end. Vander couldn't risk any more innocents getting injured or killed at the hands of the Death Lord.

The sound of a dragon's roar echoed in the air around them.

*Feno.*

Vander pounced on the tail of the Death Lord,

halting his flight into the air. The dragon turned, trying to swipe his sharp talons at Vander.

Feno flew overhead and breathed his fire down onto the dragon. Vander did the same. Dragon's fire was one way to kill another dragon. Not many knew this, and dragons did not share this information. Normal fire did nothing, but it was the magic laced into a dragon's fire that was deadly to another dragon.

Gamair tried to fight them off, but he was growing weaker by the second. They continued to breathe their flames onto him. Vander let the dragon's tail go and concentrated on sending his flames. Gamair was quickly losing his fight. He slowly tried to crawl away. Another roar came from the sky, signaling the arrival of Jodos in his dragon form. He, too, joined them in sending flames onto the black dragon. He hovered in the air alongside Feno.

Finally, the Death Lord's fight went out of him. His body collapsed to the ground, unmoving. Feno and Jodos landed, and they waited to see if the black dragon would move.

*"Is he dead?"* Jodos asked, breaking the silence through their mental link.

Vander's dragon released a growl. He moved

closer to the burnt dragon. Vander couldn't sense a heartbeat from Gamair.

*"He's dead,"* Vander informed them. His dragon huffed, pissed that it was that easy to kill the Death Lord. He would have preferred to draw out the death and torture him slowly, until he faded into nothing, but this would have to do. Short and sweet.

The villagers would now be avenged.

Dalma would be avenged.

Faye would be—

Faye! He turned his head, and his gaze frantically searched the area. He had to find her. His focus landed on the wooded area that was at the top of the hill, which led to where Gamair had appeared in the clearing. A slight movement from behind a tree caught his attention.

He slowly walked in the direction of the woods, his eyes on the small human who was peeking from behind a tree.

Faye.

*"Go to her, brother,"* Feno said. *"We'll take care of the body."*

Vander stalked toward the trees, confident his brother would do as he'd promised. Faye moved from the tree she had been hiding behind. It was the first time he had revealed his dragon to her. He had to pull back on his dragon. His beast was ready to dash over to her and scoop her up, but Vander was sure that would scare the shit out of her.

*Gentle,* he scolded his dragon. *We don't want to frighten her.*

His dragon complied and calm down slightly. They stopped just yards away from her. She stood there, eyes wide, staring up at him. She appeared so tiny standing next to his massive dragon.

"Vander?" she whispered.

Her voice was faint, but he would recognize the sound of his name on her lips anytime.

He nodded and bent down to her. His nostrils flared, and he took in her scent. No fear, just the scent of his woman. His beast loved that she was not afraid of them. Her hand touched the tip of his nose. He closed his eyes briefly, before opening them to find a whimsical smile on her lips.

"Can you understand me?" she asked.

He nodded to her. Even though his dragon was in the forefront, he was still aware of everything. He gently pushed against her hand. She had asked him before if he would take her for a ride in the sky.

Now Gamair was dead, he would be able to

finally concentrate on making her his. He leaned his head down to the ground.

She gasped and looked at him.

"A ride?" she asked, her bright smile lighting up her face. She shrieked at his nod and took off running toward him.

It was time he gave her the world.

———

Faye didn't hesitate. She ran to Vander. Her heart slammed in her chest at the sheer size of his dragon. Never would she have imagined she would watch dragons fight to the death, much less ride one. The scales that covered his body were tough but smooth to the touch. She was able to climb up on his shoulders and rested right at the base of his neck.

She braced; his muscles bunched beneath her touch before they were thrust into the air by Vander's massive wingspan. She gasped and held on tight to Vander's neck, her eyes squeezed shut. Her hair whipped around her face, and they flew through the air.

She released her grip on his neck and lifted her head slightly. With one eye open, she glanced around and saw nothing but the night sky, filled with twinkling stars. Not a cloud was in the sky, and she was in awe of what was in front of her. They glided through the peaceful night. She had never seen a sky so beautiful. It was like she had a front-row seat to a magical light show.

"This is beautiful," she murmured, opening her other eye. Excitement filled her chest, and she wished she could know what Vander was thinking. She didn't dare move. She didn't want to chance sliding off the large dragon's back.

Vander's dragon snorted, as if reading her thoughts.

"Where are we going?" she shouted around the wind. She knew it was silly to think that the dragon could respond to her.

But where were they going?

*"Home."*

The word was whispered in her ear, the breeze flying past her.

She knew they weren't heading toward Westwend. They were cutting through the sky at high speeds.

Was Vander speaking to her telepathically?

*"Whose home?"* she thought to herself. There was no way Vander was speaking to her.

No way.

"Our *home.*" His voice was now clear.

She wasn't hearing things. She sat back, amazed they were able to speak to each other. Did this mean they were truly mates? Her heart sped up at the thought. She cared deeply for him and felt there would never be another one.

"*Hold on to that thought.*" Vander's voice broke through her thoughts.

Her eyes widened; the sight of the castle came into view.

*Home.*

The large dragon circled the landing pad of the castle. She wasn't sure what to do as he made the descent toward the pad. She held on tight, and he made a soft landing. She looked around. The dragon turned and lowered itself toward the ground.

She slid off and backed away while keeping her eyes on him. She'd ridden a flipping dragon! She was in awe and stared at the dragon. The dragon returned her gaze, and appeared to puff its chest out.

She barked out a laugh, realizing he was showing off for her. Power radiated from the massive beast. He was beautiful, but she wanted to see his human counterpart.

"Such a handsome dragon. You are magnifi-cent." She smiled, clasping her hands to her chest. "But I need to speak to Vander now."

# CHAPTER NINETEEN

VANDER HAD to force his dragon to back away so he was able to shift and come to the forefront. His dragon, finally able to strut in front of Faye, was having too much fun showing off. It wanted Faye to accept him as well.

He opened his eyes, and Faye came into view. His legs moved of their own accord, needing to get to her. She ran toward him, meeting him halfway, and threw her body at him. He caught her midair, bringing her flush against his body.

"I knew you would come for me," she cried out, tightening her arms around his neck.

"Always," he whispered and promised to

never let her go. He refused to lose her and was glad Gamair was finally dead.

"Was that you in my head, or am I going crazy?" she pulled back and asked.

He smiled down at the curious look in her eye. He knew without a doubt she was his mate. If he was able to communicate telepathically with her, then that proved beyond a doubt that she was meant to be his.

"Yes," he admitted. He pushed a strand of her swamp-dried hair from her face. Even dirty from her ordeal in the Wetlands, she was the most beautiful thing he'd ever seen.

She smiled and shyly looked down, then she froze in place.

"Over time, the connection between us will get stronger."

"Oh, my goodness!" she exclaimed, shock etched on her face. "You're naked!"

He glanced down and chuckled. His cock appeared to decide to wake up at that moment and stood at attention.

"Ah, sorry," he murmured. "Clothing doesn't make it through the shift."

With a wave his hand, clothing appeared on his body, covering his naked flesh.

"Wow." Faye chuckled and eyed him. "Can

you make your clothes disappear like that, too?" She cocked an eyebrow at him.

He barked out a laugh.

He just loved her sass.

"Mine and yours," he promised. He grabbed her hand and guided her toward the entry door of the castle.

"So, what does all of this mean?" she asked and followed behind him.

It was time for him to tell her everything. That she was his mate, and that everything he had ever collected in his castle was to prepare for his mate. Now that the threat toward her was gone, they could begin their life together, as long as she would have him.

"Hold that thought." He quickly ushered her into the castle and pulled her behind him, marching down the halls. It was late at night, and most of the servants would be off duty.

"I'm sure I look like death warmed over. If my clothes are a hint of what I look like, I don't want to scare anyone—"

"You're fine. This won't take long," he assured her.

They came to the table in the hallway that blocked his hoard room. He released her hand to push the sturdy table out of the way. He turned to

Faye and blew out a nervous breath. His dragon had been collecting for years to prepare for this moment.

"Dalma told me that this room was off-limits—" she began.

He placed a finger to her lips and stared down at her.

"Come. I'll show you what's in there." He motioned for her to follow him. He stopped in front of the steel door and placed his hand on the biometric hand scanner.

Over the years, he had built up quite the hoard for his future mate. It would require top security, as technology had advanced over the years. The light over the pad on the wall beeped and went green.

Nervousness filled his chest. He opened the door. He faced her and grabbed her smaller hand into his, leading her into the room. The lights came on. They walked inside. It was a few stories tall and filled with all the treasures he'd collected over the centuries. A gasp echoed behind him, and they walked further into the room.

He turned to find her frozen in place with her eyes wide.

"Oh. My. God!" she breathed out.

Worry filled his chest. She was finally here, and

he wasn't sure if this was a good or bad reaction. He turned and scanned the rows of priceless artwork, piles of gold bricks, and shelves filled with the finest diamonds and jewels.

"Is this not good enough?" He spun back to her.

"What?" she screamed, her voice ending on a squeak. "Are you kidding me? This is amazing. Vander, how long have you been collecting this?"

"Practically all my life," he answered truthfully. He reached for her hand and came to stand near her. His heart thumped against his chest, and he stared down into her green eyes. "Faye—"

"Yes, Vander?" she whispered.

"From the moment my dragon heard your voice in that hospital room, it was drawn to you. You are who I've been collecting this treasure for. It is all for you, my mate—"

"Vander, I—"

"Please, let me finish." He placed a finger on her lips to silence her.

Her eyes softened, and she nodded.

He needed to get this off his chest. Over the centuries, he knew none of the women in the past were his mate. It would only be a matter of time before she would blow into his life and knock him on his ass. He just had to wait for that moment, only it was he who'd fallen from the sky and had been delivered to her.

"You are my mate, and dragon shifters prepare their whole lives for the day they will meet their mate. Everything I own is yours, if only you will have me."

There. He'd laid it out on the table for her. Now, panic crept up into his chest while he waited for her reply.

"Are you done?" she asked.

He nodded and again waited for her answer.

His dragon slammed into his chest, demanding to be let out. His dragon was insisting he could convince her to mate with them, but he just pushed his beast back.

"Before you cut me off, I was going to say that I don't need treasures. It's you I want. Forever."

Relief flooded him, her words sinking in. He gathered her to his chest and covered her mouth with his. Thoughts of mating with her officially crossed his mind, and he wouldn't mind consummating their mating now. She must have known where his thoughts were going.

"Vander," she gasped and drew back.

"Yes?" he questioned, nipping her bottom lip.

"I have got to take a shower. I smell like a drowned rat."

He barked out a laugh. He didn't care what she looked like. He pulled her in and wrapped his arms around her.

"Okay, stinky. Let's get you showered. We can come back so you can explore our treasure." A smile spread across his face, and he led her out of the room.

Faye Adams was the perfect mate for him. His dragon was now satisfied she had accepted them. Exploring the treasure could wait for now. It was time for him to take care of his mate.

# EPILOGUE

FAYE SMILED and rubbed her swollen belly. She was sitting at the window seat, staring at the beautiful scenery below. Aside from Dragon's Keep, she loved their penthouse condo. It had been seven months since she and Vander had completed their mating. He had come through on his promise to give her everything he owned.

It was the dragon in him, wanting to make sure she was well cared for. He'd given her not only the world but a gift that was now nestled inside her womb. Her belly jumped from the baby giving a swift kick, as if to acknowledge her rub. It had been a whirlwind mating. Her life had definitely changed for the better since making the life-long commitment with her mate.

His family had accepted her immediately, once she was introduced to them. Her family had fallen in love with Vander just as quickly as she had. They were told that Vander was a shifter, but she was unable to tell what kind to keep with the code of dragons. They were curious at first, but in the end, it didn't matter. Her family saw how much they loved each other, and they let it be.

The sound of the doorbell filled the air. She rushed from her seat to the front of the condo. In her current condition, it was more of a rushed waddle.

"It's your family," Vander called out from the foyer.

They had invited both sides of the family over for a small dinner party. Laughter floated through the air as she arrived to find her parents, Clark and Lynn, coming through the door. Her brother, River, filed in behind them.

"Daddy!" She thrust herself into her father's waiting arms. He laughed and crushed her to him, only her belly prevented them from getting closer. It had only been a week since she'd last seen her family. They were close, and she'd missed them dearly.

"Hey, pumpkin," her father greeted her with a tight squeeze.

"Oh, my! Look at that belly!" her mother exclaimed.

They gathered around her. River shook Vander's hand with a laugh.

"I know," she groaned and pulled back from her father. Her long maxi dress showcased the fullness of her growing mound.

"Hey, River." She greeted her brother with a hug.

River, unlike her, was much taller, topping over six feet.

"Hey, sis." He dropped a kiss on her forehead.

She looked around and didn't see his latest girlfriend. She cocked an eyebrow at him. He shook his head, and she knew what that meant. He was single again. Her brother went through women like a gambler went through money. One day, she hoped he would find *"the one"* and settle down.

"Dinner should be ready in a moment." She motioned toward the dining area.

Her eyes connected with Vander's. He drew closer to her. Her family's voices and laughter carried off down the hallway, and they moved into the condo.

"What are you thinking?" He gathered her into his arms.

"That I'm so thankful for you falling out of the sky," she said. Reaching up, she plucked an imaginary piece of lint from his shirt.

"I told you, when I see something I want, I go after it. You and I will be forever."

He bent his head down and covered her mouth with his. She melted against him and knew she'd better be ready. If the past year was a preview of their future, she'd better buckle up and prepare for what her dragon warrior would have in store for her.

## Note from the Author

Dear reader,

I want to thank you for the love and support. I hope you enjoyed Vander and Faye's book. I wanted to re-release this book after additional edits because I enjoyed it so much and wanted to put it in the hands of readers who I was sure would love it as well.

Please leave a review of Her Warrior Dragon on the platform you purchased it. This will help other readers decide on whether or not to grab this book and give it a try!

Best,

Ariel Marie

# About the Author

Ariel Marie is an author who loves the paranormal, action and hot steamy romance. She combines all three in each and every one of her stories. For as long as she can remember, she has loved vampires, shifters and every creature you can think of. This even rolls over into her favorite movies. She loves a good action packed thriller! Throw a touch of the supernatural world in it and she's hooked!

She grew up in Cleveland, Ohio where she currently resides with her husband and three beautiful children.

*For more information:*
www.thearielmarie.com

Also by the Author

## Dragon Mates

Her Warrior Dragon

Her Fierce Dragon

## The Dark Shadows Series

Princess

Toma

Phaelyn

Teague

Adrian

Nicu

## The Nightstar Shifters (FF shifters)

Sailing With Her Wolf

Protecting Her Wolf

Sealed With A Bite

Hers to Claim

Wanted by the Wolf

## The Immortal Reign series (FF vampires)

Deadly Kiss

Iced Heart

Royal Bite

## The Montana Grizzlies (FF Bear Shifters)

Hot For Her Bear

Claimed By Her Bear

## Blackclaw Alphas (Why Choose Series)

Fate of Four

Bearing Her Fate (TBD)

## The Midnight Coven Brand

Forever Desired

Wicked Shadows

## Paranormal Erotic Box Sets

Vampire Destiny (An Erotic Vampire Box Set)

Moon Valley Shifters Box Set (F/F Shifters)

The Dragon Curse Series (Ménage MFF Erotic Series)

## Stand Alone Books

Printed in the USA
CPSIA information can be obtained
at www.ICGtesting.com
CBHW021542100924
14345CB00029B/241

9 781956 602951